FEB 1 0 2017

Jerusalem Ablaze

Stories of Love and Other Obsessions

Jerusalem Ablaze

Stories of Love and Other Obsessions

Orlando Ortega-Medina

CLOUD
LODGE
BOOKS

First published in hardback, paperback and eBook in the UK in 2017
by Cloud Lodge Books (CLB)

A CIP catalogue record for this book is available from the British Library.

HB ISBN 978-0-9954657-0-1
PB ISBN 978-1-5262-0253-6
eBook ISBN 978-0-9954657-1-8

1 3 5 7 9 10 8 6 4 2

Print and Production Managed by
Jellyfish Solutions Ltd

Cloud Lodge Books Ltd (CLB)
38 Queen's Gate, London SW7 5HR
cloudlodgebook.com

For my life partner
ויליאם

Contents

Torture by Roses

Lasciate ogni speranza, voi ch'entrate.
    – Inferno iii, 9

Ikeda Yataro's body was cremated today. May his soul be forever damned. The flames claimed his corpse and his roses – all that was left of the man. It had been one week to the very day of his funeral that he had ended his miserable life in the most honourable way he knew.

That Ikeda killed himself is no secret. In fact, his suicide has proved to be an occasion for somber celebration within the business and artistic community. The death of yet another celebrated personage has helped keep alive the cult of honour, proof the Samurai warrior spirit is still alive in post-war Japan.

But I take another view of the matter. It's not that I'm at all put off by the idea of suicide. It's certainly a reasonable option when facing an unacceptable situation, and I admit that I myself have entertained romantic notions about the glories of an honourable death. But it is the particulars of such a death that now disturb me.

Prior to my witnessing Ikeda's suicide, I confess to having had my own little sadistic fantasies involving death; specifically, fantasies involving what I perceived to be the more erotic aspects of death.

I remember thrilling to Mishima Yukio's description of a blood-drenched soldier dying on the battlefield, of his desire to bend down to kiss the soldier's mouth as he lay gasping his last mortal breath. It was the blood that drew me.

I remember my obsessive desire to learn all the details about Mishima's own death by *seppuku*. I can recall the stinging jealousy I felt toward the young men who had enjoyed the privilege of witnessing their leader as he ripped open his belly, his bowels slipping out of the wound into a pool of his own blood. Kawabata's death by gas inhalation later that same year seemed to me an act of mere cowardice by comparison. But none of my endless ruminations could prepare me for Ikeda's suicide.

I had first heard of Ikeda when I was in my second year of primary school. He was one of those Japanese who had become a model for the post-war generation – a self-made millionaire, a phoenix who had arisen from the ashes of obscurity to the height of economic success. "As rich as Ikeda" had become a proverb with which every parent encouraged his or her child to work hard in school.

As I grew up, I came to a more complete awareness of the man. In addition to being a self-made man, Ikeda was also Japan's premier patron of the arts. He was amongst those responsible for the national preservation of traditional, courtly art forms. He was the principal patron of the Neo Kabuki. And the two main literary societies had him to thank for his generous contributions and scholarship funds. I, being an ambitious young writer, developed the profoundest respect for him.

He was rarely out of the newspapers, as it seemed certain reporters were eager to cover Ikeda's every movement. The last major story involving Ikeda was his stormy romance with the Countess Tanaka. But, as of late, Ikeda Yataro had completely dropped out of the public eye. His industrial empire was still functioning as vigorously as ever, but the man himself had all but vanished.

The rumours and speculation regarding Ikeda's disappearance abounded. Some said Ikeda had retired to a Zen monastery in a northern prefecture to live out the end of his years in quiet contemplation. Another rumour, somewhat closer to the truth, was simply that Ikeda Yataro was dead. So it was with some shock that I received the news, one morning last autumn, that the work application I had submitted at the University Housing Office was being considered by the Ikeda household. The usual arrangement was an exchange of household duties for room and board, quite common amongst university students studying far from their homes. I was summoned to an interview.

When I arrived at Ikeda's Western-style mansion in the Azabu district of Tokyo, I was somewhat taken aback by its extravagance. It was the epitome of overstated European elegance, patterned after something Greek or Roman. Its anti-Zen architecture contrasted jarringly with the other homes in the same neighbourhood, giving one the impression of a cactus planted amongst roses. I now understood the controversy that had surrounded the building of this structure.

I passed between the massive marble columns that supported the roof and, flanked on either side by twin copies of the Venus de Milo, rang the doorbell. I waited for several minutes before a woman's voice answered via the intercom system. It was Mrs Higashi, the housekeeper.

"What is it?" she said. Her voice had a grating quality that, at first hearing, I attributed to the intercom itself.

I introduced myself and informed her of my reason for coming. She was soon at the door.

Mrs Higashi led me through the maze of empty rooms that made up Ikeda's residence – as austere inside as it was excessive outside. We walked down hall after hall, deeper and higher, until I began to suspect she was leading me in a circle. She halted abruptly and turned into a small anteroom. I followed her inside.

"You will soon meet Ikeda-san," she said in her grating voice. "He will explain why you've been sent for and what will be expected of you."

I could not contain my surprise at being told I would actually be meeting Ikeda Yataro himself. Sensing this, Mrs Higashi narrowed her eyes at me and added, "Please keep your eyes on the floor. Ikeda-san does not like to be stared at. Wait here."

I was left alone for a while, and I believe I must have dozed off, for I was suddenly startled by the sliding of two immense panels at the other end of the anteroom. An overpowering flowery odour filled the room. In the doorway appeared a gaunt old man. It was Ikeda.

He stood there for a few seconds, staring at me.

"I know who you are," he said after a moment, moving languidly in my direction.

"Yes," I said, "I was sent here by the university."

"You were sent for by me."

"Yes, yes, of course by you, Ikeda-san." I bowed apologetically.

Ikeda paced the little room, never taking his eyes off me.

"I've read your work in the *Asahi Review*," he said. "It's been well received."

"Not really, Ikeda-san."

"No?" he said with mock surprise. "I understand you received a fellowship at the university based on the merits of your work."

"I'm not exactly sure on what criteria the final decision was based. Perhaps it was my poetry. I don't know."

Ikeda stopped his pacing and faced me. I looked down.

"Your poetry ..." Ikeda's lips drew back into a vague smile. "I like to read poetry, and I like to keep up with new writers published in the *Asahi Review*. I own it, you know."

"Yes, Ikeda-san."

I felt an odd mix of awe and caution standing in Ikeda's presence. Here was a man who had accomplished more in one lifetime than a hundred others could ever hope for. One could not help but admire him. And yet there was an almost palpable decadence that hung about his person. I couldn't identify it exactly, but the effect was less than pleasant and, try as I might, I could not shake it off.

"Your poems are quite delicate," he said. "You write with the profoundest sense of beauty, with precision, yes, even with a kind of boldness. And yet beneath the surface of your beautiful words I perceive a hint of darkness, something ominous that breaks through to the surface every now and again. Am I right? Please don't answer. Of course, you probably don't even realise these things yourself just yet.

"At first I thought my own misreading was causing me to interpret your words in this way, so I reread your poems several times. I came to the definite conclusion that the darkness is there, groaning to break out of its beautiful confines, desiring to ooze up between those delicate words and overwhelm this beatific vision of yours."

When he finished speaking, I raised my eyes a bit; Ikeda was staring at me with hard, almost hateful eyes. Had he summoned me only to mock my writing, or was he truly an admirer of my work?

"Ikeda-san, forgive me," I said after a few moments of awkward silence. "I'm sure you overestimate my abilities –"

"Nonsense!" he said, "It's you who do not yet understand the implications of your work. But that is neither here nor there. You see, this is precisely the reason I've summoned you. The fact is, I have chosen you to be my heir."

I looked up at Ikeda in utter shock. He returned my look with such fierceness that I had to look back down at the floor. I was sure the man had turned lunatic. He paced the room with increasing frenzy, dramatically punctuating his words with his hands.

I tried to keep my eyes on the floor as instructed, but I could hardly keep from noticing the strange markings running the length of Ikeda's calves, showing intermittently each time he kicked up the bottom of his bathrobe.

"Young man, I am in need of a confessor. I believe that in you I have finally found someone who may be able to understand my soul. I want to pour into you all that I am. I want to ravish that virgin spirit of youthful naiveté surging through your poems."

"Ikeda-san," I said, "surely you can't ravish that which willingly yields." I didn't know what I was saying, but somehow Ikeda's deep interest in me was beginning to intoxicate me with its possibilities, regardless of its irrationality.

Ikeda halted his pacing and flashed a row of yellow teeth. "You are right, young man. I cannot ravish, but I can have, if you are indeed willing ..."

I was at a complete loss for words. Ikeda sensed my dismay.

"Think seriously about my offer, young man. The benefits are great. Only one will be able to claim he is Ikeda's heir, and that one could be you."

His eyes widened and his mouth hung open a bit as he waited for a response.

"Suppose that I accepted your offer," I said. "What would I have to do ... besides merely to allow your indulgence?"

Ikeda eyed me, as if memorising every physical detail about me.

"Your duties would be simple; I have few needs. As you are probably already aware, I never leave this house. You need only bring me my meals and any correspondence that might happen to arrive for me. The rest of your time here will belong to you, to do with as you wish. Besides this, I have three rules you must promise to observe. The first is that you ask me no questions. If you have any, I will know and will answer them in good time. The second is that you must do everything I ask of you. You need not worry yourself over this. I will never ask you to do anything that would compromise your morals. Your morals will become my morals anyway. In any event, I will never touch you, and you will never have the need to touch me, with the exception of one time. You will know when the time comes.

"If you violate either of these rules, you forfeit our arrangement and will be asked to leave.

"The third rule is that you tell no one of our arrangement until I release you to do so. Tell no one that you've even seen me. I will leave the details of your deception to you.

"If you decline, I trust you will ensure that the confidence with which I've entrusted you will remain our secret. If you decide to accept my offer, you will move in straight away."

The following day I returned and accepted Ikeda's offer – on his terms.

—∞—

The first morning, I took my meal alone in the immense marbled dining area overlooking the gardens. I was in the midst of pondering the sudden change in my circumstances, when Mrs Higashi appeared and placed a tray of food on the table next to me. I rose to my feet.

"Good morn –"

"Take this to Ikeda-san. Place it outside his room and knock once on his door. Then come back and take him his post. You'll find it in the entryway." She turned to leave.

"Wouldn't it be easier to do both at the same time?"

She turned back. "I've been here for five years," she said, and walked away.

I decided to maintain the status quo, at least for the present, and followed her instructions.

When I arrived at the entryway to collect Ikeda's post, I found that the only thing there was a flower box, the kind used to send roses.

I brought the long box up to Ikeda's room and noticed that his food was still outside the door. I knocked, softly at first.

There was no answer, so I knocked once again, this time more forcefully. Again there was no answer, only the sound of a faint stirring emanating from behind the door.

"Ikeda-san," I called.

"Come in," I heard him say faintly.

I slid open the door panel and was overcome by a strong perfume – the same odour I had encountered the previous afternoon. I stepped into the large, windowless room, illumined only by four flickering votive candles, one in each corner. What I saw inside tore my heart. The room was devoid of furniture, save for an immense, black lacquered dressing chest pushed against the far wall. Atop the chest sat a delicate crystal vase containing a single blood-red rose. It had already begun to wither. The floor of the room was carpeted with hundreds, perhaps thousands, of horned stems, corpses of roses arranged meticulously into hexagrams reminiscent of the I Ching. In the midst of these sat Ikeda, his back turned to me, sitting cross-legged, and wearing only a loincloth.

Ikeda, hardly acknowledging my presence, raised his arm and pointed a trembling finger at the chest.

"Replace the rose in the vase with the one in the box," he said in a dreadful monotone. "Do it now."

Barefoot, I picked my way through the thorns. I glanced at Ikeda's back as I passed him and was struck with horror. It was covered with scars, old and new, places where his skin had evidently been pierced through by thorns. Some of the wounds oozed freely.

I caught my breath and moved quickly to my task, replacing the old rose with the new, then stood there stupidly, not knowing what to do next – careful not to enquire of Ikeda, lest I violate my agreement to refrain from asking questions.

"Find a place for the old one," he said.

Even though he had spoken to me, he never moved his eyes from the vase. He stared at the new rose, slack-jawed, with the most pained expression I had ever seen on any man's face. I wondered what could have brought this great man to so wretched a condition.

Placing the rose in a corner, I moved reverently out of the room and slid shut Ikeda's coffin lid.

That night, as I lay on my bed, imprisoned between wakefulness and limbo, I imagined Ikeda stretched out to sleep on his bed of thorns, candles blazing around him. I tried to extinguish the ghastly image of the man from my mind, but it refused to fade.

This went on day after day, week after week. Ikeda rarely left his room and barely acknowledged my presence. A rose would arrive each morning; Ikeda would receive it in his room – no explanations.

—⟋⟍—

One night, as I lay in the midst of a fitful sleep, I opened my eyes and found myself staring up at Ikeda's face, cadaverous in the semidarkness of the room. He was gazing down at me as if in a trance.

"Ikeda-san …"

"Say nothing," he whispered.

I closed my eyes. I could feel his hot breath on my face, my chest. After a moment he was gone.

I wondered how long he had been coming into my room to watch me. As time went on, I became aware of his presence on other occasions. Just knowing he was there, or would soon arrive to hover over me, made it nearly impossible to fall asleep. Somehow I managed to keep my eyes closed, pretending to sleep.

During the days that followed, whenever the weather permitted, I took long walks in the park, trying to purge myself of the unease I was experiencing. Soon, however, with the advance of the winter rains, I was forced to stay indoors and face the choice I had made. It seemed a small enough price to pay to claim the privilege of being Ikeda's adopted heir.

—⁂—

Perhaps it was a month later that Ikeda's voice awakened me. He was urgently calling me to his room over the intercom system. I pulled on my housecoat and ran down the dark hall to see what was wrong.

When I arrived, I found Ikeda in the middle of his room standing next to a full-length mirror.

"Come to me," he said.

I hesitated a moment, looking down at the thorns, then moved toward him, trying my best to avoid injuring my bare feet.

As I drew close to him, Ikeda thrust his index finger toward the mirror. "Stand there, face the mirror, and remove all your clothing."

I don't know if it was exhaustion, fear, or greed that kept me from fleeing Ikeda's presence right then and there. But whatever the reason, a moment later I found myself dropping my house-coat to the floor and facing my naked reflection in Ikeda's mirror. Ikeda caught his breath and backed away, crushing a half dozen dried-out, thorny stems with his bare feet as he retreated.

"I am going to paint a portrait of you, my young man," he said, and moved behind the mirror.

I stood for several seconds staring at my reflection, wondering what he was doing. I could hear his loud breathing. Then he grasped the mirror and moved it aside. I found myself suddenly face-to-face with him. He stared at me intensely as if in an act of meditation.

"You think I'm an invert, but you're wrong," he said as he dropped his loincloth to the floor. I had to look away.

"Open your eyes. I am your mirror now. Behold yourself."

I opened my eyes.

"You are so young. Your skin is smooth and tight." His voice took on a satirical tone. "Why, you're almost glowing." He moved closer. "Perhaps the vision of beauty evident in your poetry proceeds from your youthful body. Your … fragile body. What do you think?"

"I don't know, Ikeda-san," I said. "I write what I feel."

"You're lying," he said. "Are you afraid to speak the truth to me? To yourself? About what inspires you?"

"I'm not lying. I write what I feel, nothing more."

"Well, then your feelings are much darker than even you yourself are aware. Darker than any of the pastiche you manage to squeeze out on the page. Don't you think I can see that?"

"I thought you liked my work."

"What I like is the potential I see in both your work and in you. That is why you are here. I have work to do."

I forced myself to look directly into Ikeda's eyes. As our eyes met, he inclined his head toward me and said: "Most people have to wait until their bodies begin to age, until they themselves begin to turn ugly, before they can give up their ridiculous notions about beauty. But you are fortunate. Now you have me for your mirror."

He moved to within an inch of my face.

"Why, you're practically flawless," he whispered. He knelt before me. "Flawless … But this," he said, moving upward until his face was directly opposite my appendix scar. His eyes glistened. "This is your most attractive feature."

He stood and moved around behind me. I could feel his stale breath hot on my neck.

"Stop your trembling. It's unbecoming."

"Yes, Ikeda-san."

"Tell me, do you have a girl?"

"Yes, Ikeda-san, back home in Kagoshima."

"How long have you known each other?"

"Since we were children. Our fathers are business associates."

"Do you love her?"

"Very much …"

"I want you to leave her."

"Ikeda-san …"

"Is something wrong?"

"What you ask is … is not easy."

"Have you so soon forgotten our agreement?"

"It's just that it's a formal engagement."

"Yes, I understand all that," Ikeda said, barely containing his scorn. "You needn't worry, young man. I'm all the family you'll need now. Trust me."

"It isn't just that," I said.

"Well, then what?"

"We love each other."

Ikeda drew a deep breath.

"Listen, my young man, it's good to love," he said. "But it's also good to hate." He lingered on the word. "If you don't know how to hate, then you are only half a person. Do you know how to hate, young man?"

I could feel him breathing harder.

"I think so," I said.

"No, I don't believe you do. You would know with more certainty if you did," he said. "Pay close attention to what I'm about to say to you. Love is pleasant enough, but it's just a sedative. Hate, on the other hand, is invigorating. It's good to plunge into the iciness of hate after languishing in the drowsy heat of love."

I was starting to feel exhausted. The room seemed to be tipping up at an angle. And yet Ikeda continued his relentless diatribe.

"Everyone speaks about love's passion. Let me tell you, love's passion is no match for the passion of hate."

He spoke with such authority that I could not help listening to him. I felt repelled, and yet at the same time there was something compelling about his words. I felt myself being drawn into his world.

"Have you ever felt real passion, young man?"

"No, sir ... never any real passion."

"Would you like to learn to hate?"

I wanted to say, "Yes, Ikeda-san, teach me to hate," but the words wouldn't come. Some inner barrier prevented me from revealing my desires.

"Why are you sweating, young man?"

"I want to ... please ... I don't know ..."

"Don't hesitate, young man. Let me be your guide." He moved around to face me. I looked away. "Come, young man, don't wait. Seize the opportunity."

"Please, Ikeda-san, I'm tired. Please let me rest now."

There was an interminable silence. Two of the candles had gone out. Ikeda backed away.

"Go then," he said, "go to bed and think about what we've discussed. Perhaps tomorrow."

I pulled on my housecoat, went to my room and jumped into bed. Part of me wanted to run away, to be done with Ikeda. But another part, the stronger part, was experiencing a symbiosis. In my heart of hearts I knew that I had begun to feed on Ikeda's misery as much as he was feeding on me. Within minutes I fell dead asleep.

—⁓—

The train ride to Kagoshima was a journey through a kind of thick fog. A sense of vagueness lay over the countryside as it flew past my window. Only once was my vision of the landscape disturbed, and that when the train plunged headlong into the undersea tunnel connecting the island of Honshu with the island of Kyushu. I felt momentarily trapped, unable to breathe easily. The palms of my hands broke out into a sweat and my pulse raced. I rose from my seat and paced the car. My thoughts were only of escape. Why had I come? What would I say to her?

The conductor asked me to sit down but someone had taken my seat, and I spent the remainder of the journey holding on to an overhead strap.

As the train neared Kagoshima, I was overcome with an incredible apprehension. No matter what explanation I gave her, there was nothing I could say to allay the disgrace both our families would experience. I kept asking myself if this was what I really wanted.

When our train arrived at Nishi-Kagoshima station, I could see her standing on the platform, her bright-yellow dress contrasting sharply with the drab surroundings. Anxiety was clearly etched on her face, as she searched the horde stepping off the train.

It had been six months since we had last seen each other. Everything had gone so well between us. Our engagement had been approved by both our families, and we had spent long evenings together talking about our future life. We had kept in constant contact by post but, in the three months I had spent with Ikeda, my letter writing had dropped off to almost nothing. I just didn't have the energy any longer. Finally, I had sent her the telegram:

Meet me tomorrow at Nishi-Kagoshima station. 10am,
Platform 5. Important.

I stepped off the train, moved quickly in her direction and took hold of her wrist. Without protesting, she trailed behind until I pulled her into one of the sordid little coffee shops bordering the station.

"Your hands are so cold," I heard her say.

"It's the weather," I said, avoiding her eyes.

"It's much colder in Tokyo."

We sat next to each other in a corner booth surrounded by vagrants and minor businessmen who gulped down tea and ran out the door to catch their trains. I could feel her searching my face for some clue as to the reason I had cabled her, whilst I continued to avoid looking at her, considering what I was going to say next.

Finally, I clenched my teeth, turned my head and stared at her. She blinked at me for a moment and then looked away, her eyes moist, waiting passively as does a lamb for the inevitable slash of the butcher's knife. Her innocence unsettled me. I felt insulted and angered by it. How dare she exhibit this purity of spirit in a world so devoid of anything pure. At last I realised I had made the proper decision.

"Imoto-san, I must call off our engagement."

She looked back at me quickly, then her hand shot out and came to rest on my arm.

"But, my family ..."

"I sent them a letter this morning explaining everything."

A slight tremor passed through her body, and she slid closer to me. Her eyes projected such sadness that they could have melted the coldest of hearts. But they had no such effect on me. Quite to the contrary, I was beginning to enjoy this exchange. The feeling crept over me, gradually easing away the tension I had been feeling since the beginning of our meeting. There was something suddenly liberating about watching this girl's world crumbling around her.

"Do you ... do you need more time? I can wait ..."

"No. Go find someone else."

Her grip tightened on my arm and, in that grip, I felt her silent desperation. It excited me to see her this way, to feel her suffering.

"Don't you ..." Her eyes filled with tears. "Don't you love me?" she said.

"I never loved you, Imoto. I only felt sorry for you."

I could hear Ikeda voicing his approval: Yes, young man. That's the way.

The tears were now flowing freely down her face. I had to suppress the urge to smile.

"Please ..." she said.

"Let go of my arm now, Imoto."

She relaxed her grip. I got up, slapped a 10,000-yen note on the table, and swaggered out of the shop with just enough time to catch the 10.30 train back to Tokyo.

—ⵣⵣ—

Over the next few weeks I noticed my feelings of triumph giving way to a sense of melancholy. It was as if a shroud were being slowly drawn over my heart. At first, it was nothing serious, just a general feeling of listlessness. I found it increasingly difficult to concentrate on my studies, and I almost never wrote any more. Soon after, I began shunning the company of friends at school, eager to escape the sunlit grounds of the university, always alive with people, to bury myself in the deathly stillness of Ikeda's mausoleum.

The storms came and winter blanketed the island of Honshu in ice. And as the winter took hold, Ikeda experienced a renaissance of sorts, exchanging places with me in the land of the living.

For some unexplained reason, he began to put in appearances at the Neo Kabuki, occupying the seat of honour in the founder's box. He also made several presentations, including the prestigious Mainichi Award for best film. Often I would lie on my bed, watching him on television, the crowds clamouring to steal a look at the elusive man. He always wore an inscrutable serpent's smile. I felt as if he were consciously mocking me.

Each time he returned home after spending the evening at one of these events, it fell upon me to help peel off his clothes – clothes that had adhered to his oozing wounds. I believe it was at moments like these that he became aware of my increasing distaste for him for, soon afterward, he began punishing me, playing senseless little games with me. Those were the evenings when he would call for me:

"Young man, come here quickly."

I would rush to see what he needed only have him dismiss me with a perfunctory, "Nothing."

Episodes like this would sometimes last for hours.

"Young man."

"Yes, Ikeda-san ..."

"Nothing."

"Young man ..."

"Yes ...?"

"Nothing."

After a while I would end up ignoring his calls and fall asleep to the sound of his voice droning over the intercom system, ad infinitum.

"Young man, come here ..."

"Young man ..."

"Young man ..."

I wanted to wrench his head from his neck. Eventually he tired of this and thought up new games with which to torment me.

I was slated to take my qualifying examinations in less than two months. Having chosen Chikamatsu's *Love Suicides* as my subject, I plunged into my research in earnest. Ikeda, piqued at my waning interest in his tutelage, complained loudly. His abusiveness was becoming absolutely unbearable.

—⁓—

April brought the cherry blossoms and a growing resolve on my part to resist any further incursion of Ikeda's will into my soul. At first, I had to force myself to leave the house. I started slowly. Walking alone, along the broad avenue bordering the Imperial

Palace, I took in the advancing warmth of the spring. I sought refuge in the library, in parks, at the homes of friends.

At the height of the cherry blossom viewing season, I decided one evening, at the prompting of some classmates, to join a group of them at Chidorigafuchi – the Abyss of a Thousand Birds – a long narrow park bordering the Imperial Palace moat, for the largest viewing party of the season. Hundreds of us gathered underneath the trees, their blossom-laden branches illumined by traditional paper lanterns. We ate and drank and sang. It was a good time, and yet I could not quite feel a part of it. It was as if I were watching it all from high up through my window at Ikeda's house. I wanted desperately to feel something of the bond that joined my friends together, and the secret knowledge that I was Ikeda's heir was fast becoming thin comfort.

As the celebration wore to an end, the desire to stay behind possessed me. The crowds dispersed, my friends went home, the attendants extinguished the lanterns and I was left alone. Occasional gusts of wind picked up paper cups and napkins, hurling them in the darkness across the park. I was determined not to go home that night.

Moving across the damp grass, I strolled over to a dense grove of cherry trees standing next to the palace wall. I was getting sleepy and curled up at the foot of the largest tree. A chill blew off the moat, and I was taken with uncontrollable shivering. Looking around, I found a bundle of discarded newspaper lying nearby. Carefully, I worked with the paper until I had made for myself a provisional sort of blanket. After lying down once more, I soon fell asleep.

Sometime in the middle of the night, I was awakened by a rustling sound near my head. Opening my eyes, I sensed someone bending over me. I reached out and grabbed hold of a thin wrist. Pulling it toward me, I found myself looking into the face of an attractive middle-aged woman, elegantly dressed in an exquisite silk kimono. Her eyes were wide but unalarmed.

I was taken with a desire to have the woman. Pulling her down, I kissed her hard on the mouth. She put up no resistance. My heart beat wildly, the blood surged to my head and I pushed her away. Her willingness frightened me. Getting up, I tore out of the park and never stopped running until, exhausted, I fell like a dead man on my bed.

—⁂—

The day came, some weeks later, that the flow of roses stopped. I informed Ikeda, and he seemed mildly annoyed but not at all disturbed.

When I arrived at university that morning, the campus was ablaze with the news that the Count and Countess Tanaka had been killed in an automobile accident on the Tokyo-Osaka motorway the night before. Their vehicle had spun out of control on the slick road and had gone careening over the cliffs into the ocean. It was a national calamity. The Tanakas were members of one of Japan's oldest houses and the countess was carrying their first child.

Classes were held in a spirit of sober introspection. It was the day of my oral examinations but I was in no mood to speak. As I sat at a desk, putting my notes in order, my name was called over the public-address system. The examiners looked up at me curiously. They knew as well as I did that the public-address system was used only in cases of dire emergency.

I pushed through the throngs of students and visitors jamming the halls. It felt good to make physical contact with other people, to feel like a human being again.

When I arrived at the university administration office, the secretary in charge of student affairs told me that there was an emergency at the Ikeda household and that the housekeeper had called for me to return home, specifically stating that the matter was of the gravest urgency.

I rushed out of the office, angry that my examinations had to be postponed. I could not imagine what could possibly be so important that it could not wait until the afternoon. And yet, Ikeda was not in the habit of risking unneeded suspicion by calling me at school.

I arrived at Ikeda's in a matter of minutes, dashed up to his room, slid open the door panel without knocking and stepped inside. The room was stifling. All the roses had been swept up and piled into a large heap in one corner of the room. Ikeda stepped into the room behind me, wrapped in a black winter coat, as if he were stepping into an icebox. His breath condensed in the air as he spoke.

"I've sent home Mrs Higashi. She won't be needed any more."

"That's your business. Why did–?"

"I'm embarking on a journey."

"Why did you call me out of class?"

Ikeda looked momentarily startled but soon recovered. "You agreed not to ask questions."

"Shit on our agreement."

Ikeda held his place steadily. His eyes narrowed as he spoke. "I'll ignore that little indiscretion."

"That is entirely up to you."

He edged closer to me and his voice fell to a whisper. "Countess Tanaka is dead," he said.

"Yes, I heard."

His eyes looked dull. They seemed to be covered by a thin film of mucus. He looked tentatively at the heap of stems rotting in the corner.

"The roses ... they were from the Countess Tanaka?" I asked.

"No questions," he whispered.

"You told me you would answer my questions."

"I told you that your questions would be answered. That's quite a different matter." He walked to the heap of dead roses. "As long as the countess lived, there was some hope ..."

"Hope? You speak of hope? All the time you were bent on destroying in me any hope of beauty or of love, you ... you secretly held on to it for yourself?"

Ikeda stood stone mute. I had never seen him at such a loss for words.

"You know, Ikeda, you are really quite pitiful." I turned on my heels to leave.

"Young man, stop, please ..."

"What do you want?"

"Young man, do you love me?"

"No. I hate you."

Ikeda's lips parted, revealing a sick smile.

"You're a good student," he whispered.

"You've been an excellent teacher."

"Tell me," he said, reaching into the pocket of his housecoat, "do you hate me enough to kill me?" He withdrew an antique ritual knife and offered it to me. It glinted in the candlelight.

"Of course not."

"Then I'll have to do it myself." He edged closer.

"You're bluffing. You haven't got the courage to kill yourself."

"Haven't I?" Ikeda held out the knife to me. "Perhaps you can show me how it's done."

"Stop playing with me, Ikeda. I'm liable to put you in hospital."

Ikeda shrugged and absently turned the knife over in his hands. "When it's over, ring my lawyers. You'll find their business card on my dresser." He paused and pulled a 10,000-yen note out of his housecoat. "Here's a little something for you, for all your trouble. Good luck."

"But, I thought ... what about the ...?"

"Your inheritance?" he said. "Didn't you know? I've been feeding it to you all along, little by little. It's inside you. It's me."

"You bastard."

"What's wrong? You don't feel cheated, do you?"

"You damned son of a bitch."

"There was one more thing I wanted you to have."

"What?"

"I'm your mirror, remember?" he said, raising the knife to his throat. "Behold your death."

"Ikeda-san, don't …!"

Ikeda savagely carved open his throat with one sweep of the blade. I rushed forward. The pressure in his body sent a hot stream of blood shooting across the room, hitting me in the face. There was nothing I could do except hold him as I was bathed head to foot in sticky blood. I watched helplessly as it collected in pools and spread out into the corners of the room. The air grew heavy with a suffocating odour and still the yawning wound continued to pour forth the steaming blood. As the muscles of his body relaxed, Ikeda's corpse let loose a rush of excrement.

What honour, what dignity in death!

I lowered the body to the floor and cradled the half-severed head on my lap. I sat staring at the pool of blood as it grew larger on the polished wood floor. I bent down and, with my finger, idly traced Ikeda's name in the dark red, congealing ink of his blood.

I sat there, numb, as the postmortem spasms abated into stillness. And then I looked down at him again.

Had this truly been the great Ikeda? No. The Ikeda of my youth had passed from this world long ago. He lived only in the memory of those who had admired and found inspiration in him. I had never known that Ikeda. I had known, only too well, the residue of a great man who had once existed. Nothing more.

I got up abruptly and let the body fall to the floor. The head made a loud thump as it struck the wood. It didn't matter.

I slid across the floor and went to the study to telephone Ikeda's lawyers. They had received a telegram from him earlier that morning, explaining his intentions. I found it strange that no one had tried to stop him. Ikeda was right: his lawyers took care of everything – efficiently and impersonally. And I was left with nothing except 10,000 yen and the desire to grind Ikeda's face into the ground with the heel of my foot.

Goddamn you to hell, Ikeda Yataro. I spit on your grave. May hope be forever banished from your soul. I pray that you be caught in an endless cycle of misery.

As for me, the torture is over. You wounded me, Ikeda, but you were never able to completely reave me of my hope. Though I still bleed, I have this consolation: fresh wounds, in later years, often make interesting scars.

Eyesore in the Ginza

Today was the first time I ever saw a beggar. It was a pretty disgusting sight, too. He was lying in the little alleyway between our dentist's office and the liquor store. I think he was an American but I'm not really sure. He sure wasn't Japanese.

What kind of bothered me was that here was this dirty *hakujin*, sprawled in our nice clean Ginza alley, making a real eyesore of himself. He was dressed all in rags, like you'd expect – except for his shoes. Those really stood out. A pair of black leather Louis Vuitton high-top trainers (the kind I like), and they looked brand new.

Now I know what you're probably thinking. What, you might ask, would a stinking beggar be doing smack in the middle of the Ginza anyway, a thorn on the rose of our neighbourhood? Well, that's exactly what I asked myself. As I stood there, thinking this over, he suddenly opened his eyes. I was startled for a moment; he was more startled.

In a flip-flash, I slugged him over the head with my book bag. He lunged forward. I smacked him again. This time his head hit the brick wall behind him, and he went out like a video game in tilt.

I quickly stooped down and untied the shoes. My hands worked furiously, pulling here and tugging there. A couple of times, I gagged on the tramp's stench. He reeked of sake and garlic. Just as I yanked the shoes off the louse, a gurgly sound came out of his throat. I thought he was about to reboot, so I beaned him again. His face went splat into the gutter.

I had the shoes in my book bag so fast that I could've beat the bullet train in a race, and just in time, too. I could hear my mom yelling out my name. She was done with her dentist appointment. I think she got fitted with some new dentures or something. She'd be pretty sore at me, since I hadn't waited in the lounge like I was supposed to.

I didn't care. I had a new pair of shoes.

After the Storm

The cold eye of the sun seared through thick layers of clouds after the storm. From the lighthouse on the promontory it appeared as a luminous disk barely the size of a half dollar, but a welcome sight nonetheless to the young woman barricaded inside, because it heralded the end of a week-long quarantine. Down below, the ocean continued to vomit forth waves of foam and debris on to the beach.

A war of light and shadow was taking place at the eastern edge of the sky. Clouds were amassing once again into a tower of moisture, slowly changing from grey into black. Out of this mass of cumulonimbus, seabirds descended in a mad spiral, only to be caught up again in the violent updrafts. A flock of gulls returned to the shoreline to pick at dead fish and sand crabs, the spoils of the storm, which lay amongst the mounds of seaweed, strewn about on the sand.

As the early-morning mists continued to burn off, the young woman unbolted the door and stepped out of the lighthouse. She was immediately whipped around by the gale. Pulling tight her overcoat, she faced into the wind, moved resolutely to an indentation in the side of the cliff, and started down the rocks to the beach.

She was familiar with every crag, every toehold, and she mechanically worked her way down rock by rock, boulder by boulder, to the shoreline, keeping her widening eyes fixed on a massive mound of seaweed that had washed ashore during the storm.

The young woman had seen an infinite abundance of sea-weed in her many years as the wife of a lighthouse keeper. But this particular mound disturbed her in its size, in its shape. She had first spotted it through the mists in the early hours of the morning as she surveyed the beach from the tower on behalf of her absent husband. At first, she had thought it might be the carcass of a grey whale. But as the mist burned off, she could see clearly that it was only a large mound of seaweed. Still, she had felt the pangs of something vaguely ominous. And as her husband was not there to reassure her, having been kept away by the fury of the storm, she decided to investigate on her own.

As she reached the sand, she stopped for a moment to consider the shoreline. It was a particularly beautiful, rock-strewn strip of the Oregon coast, fringed by a heavily wooded area. The trees of the forest seemed to march en masse into the water, stopped short by a forbidding ribbon of bone-grey sand. The beach itself ended a half-mile down but the trees continued up a rocky cliff and into the distance as far as one could see.

The strange mass of seaweed lay well onshore near the cliff-side at the opposite end of the beach from the woman. A flash of prickly heat surged into her face. She brought her cold, chapped hands to her cheeks and closed her eyes. *Please, God,* she thought, *let it be nothing.*

Her prayer was answered by a blast of icy wind that drove her from behind. She stumbled forward in the direction of the mound, never taking her eyes off it. *What will I do when I get there?* she thought.

The woman's breathing shallowed as she drew nearer and she soon felt light-headed. A breaker exploded against a large rock formation, spraying her with sticky salt water. She did not bother to wipe her face. Instead, she pressed forward across the sand. She felt a sharp pain in her hands. Looking down at them she saw that she had bitten her fingernails to the cuticles. They were bleeding. She stuffed her hands back inside the pockets of her coat and continued forward.

Scores of seabirds descended to feed on the mound. Two gulls savaged a fish head in a mad tug-of-war, oblivious of the woman who had come within a few feet of the mound. Her heart was pounding, seeking to break the bounds of her chest.

"Shoo, birds ..." she whispered.

The birds ignored the woman. They converged on the middle of the mound and pecked at it aggressively. Their frenzy upset the woman.

"Shoo, birds!" she said, louder.

Still the birds continued to feed. The woman looked around and spotted a large piece of driftwood. She shifted to pick it up, when something caught her eye and stopped her in mid motion. Next to it lay a gold chain, half-buried in the sand. The woman reached out and extracted it. From the chain dangled a little cross. She brushed it clean, then held it up to the waning light. On the cross was an engraving:

For my beloved son Michael on the day of his confirmation.
Love, your father. 11/30/97

Glancing around furtively, she slipped the necklace into a side pocket of her coat and snatched up the piece of driftwood.

"Go away, birds!" she screamed, hurling it into the midst of the flock.

The gulls dispersed with a general shriek of protest, leaving the mound free for the woman's inspection. Keeping a respectful distance, she moved in a half circuit around the mound. She soon realised, with a slowly growing sense of relief, that her apprehension had been unfounded, as there appeared to be nothing unusual about the mound aside from its size. The woman closed her eyes, took a few deep, calming breaths, then picked up her pace to complete the circuit, now keen to return to the security of the lighthouse.

Stepping quickly around the side of the mound exposed to the water, she caught her foot on something, lost her balance, and fell face down on the cold, wet sand. Temporarily dazed, she was soon revived by a sheet of ocean water gliding onshore. Moving on to her knees, she turned to see what had caused her fall. There, sticking out about a half foot from the seaweed, was the unmistakable form of a human hand.

All the apprehension that had been building within the woman since the early morning came crashing down on her again in a wave of horror. The instinct to flee overcame her but she was unable to will her body away. Instead, she edged nearer the appendage. It was obviously the hand of a man, palm down in the sand, though it was difficult to tell at first because of the places around the knuckles where the flesh had been pecked away by the birds.

The stiff fingers seemed to be straining to reach for something in the tide that now churned, now receded around the hand. Tiny sand crabs scurried along the wrist and into the folds of debris. The woman, who a moment before had been held in the grip of a psychic paralysis, now felt a kind of fascination begin to compete with her terror. It drew her forward.

The tide pushed in again, this time a few inches higher up on the beach, partially bathing the piebald hand. As the water receded, little eddies were formed by the fingers in the foam. Pulling out her own warm hand from inside her overcoat, the woman reached out and pressed her fingers against the lifeless flesh. *Strange,* she thought, *it doesn't feel that much different from the hand of a living person. I've been more alarmed by my own hand when it's fallen asleep during the night.*

A cold blast of wind and spray pulled her out of her meditation and back to the unpleasant reality before her. *Someone has to be notified,* she thought. She stood and surveyed the shoreline. She knew there was no one around for at least 50 miles but she looked anyway. She thought of the shortwave radio back at the lighthouse.

A screech behind her startled her. The gulls were returning to feed. Running up, she screamed and waved her arms in a vain effort to scare away the birds. *I can't just leave him here,* she thought.

"I won't leave you," she said out loud.

She sat on a rock, trying to decide what to do. Out of the corner of her eye she could see the hand sticking out so conspicuously, she wondered how she could have ever missed seeing it as she had approached.

Overhead the wind raked a bank of clouds across the face of the sun, and the temperature seemed to drop a full 10 degrees. The woman drew her overcoat tightly about her and dug deep into the pockets. Her left hand made contact with the gold chain, reminding her of the inscription.

"For my beloved son ..." she whispered.

Something tightened in her chest as she made the connection between the chain and the hand.

"Michael ..."

Suddenly the hand had an identity, and that identity was someone's beloved son, whose body was connected to that hand – and the body that was someone's son was lying buried underneath a pile of seaweed and rubbish and ...

The woman rushed forward, falling with a splash on her knees in front of the hand. Kneeling in the shallow water, she began to tremble. She reached out once again and held on to the hand.

"No, Michael ... I won't leave you here."

With a resoluteness that would have been impossible moments before, the woman worked methodically to free the body from the tangle of seaweed.

Twenty minutes later she found herself staring down at the bloated corpse of a young man. He had been poorly dressed for the kind of weather they had been having for the past few weeks, just a thin pair of white cotton trousers and a blood red corduroy shirt. The woman drew back and took in a slow, even breath.

Brushing away a few strands of hair that had fallen across her face, she gazed at the young man. There was something familiar about his face. Perhaps, she thought, it was only the expression it wore.

A half hour later the woman stood at the foot of the promontory, having managed to drag the young man's body across the sand. Her chest was heaving and she mopped the sweat, which was now pouring freely down her face, with the back of her hand. Her eyes traced the long scar of black sand she had carved along the edge of the beach by dragging the body. The cicatrix would soon be covered and washed away by the advancing tide, erasing all traces of her effort.

She sat down next to the corpse in an effort to catch her breath. Looking down at its face, it seemed to her that its expression had changed. It looked sadder to her, like the face of a child about to burst into tears. She brushed away a matted lock of hair that had fallen across its face.

"There now," she said, "once I get you inside, you'll be all right."

A few raindrops made cool contact with her burning skin. She gazed out over the sea as a few heavy drops pierced the skin of the water. The rain felt as if it was boring its way into her soul. Then for a moment, a very brief moment, she thought she heard someone call her name.

Susan ...

The name seemed to float, hovering tentatively on the sea air. The woman looked up. In the 30 minutes that had passed, the sky had quilted over to the horizon with thunder-packed clouds. Everything had become strangely quiet, a stillness broken only by the crash of waves on the rocks. Even the ever-present wind had died down and, in the silence, the woman again heard her name.

Susan ...

She looked down curiously at the young man's face. All traces of its sadness had disappeared. Its bluish lips had parted in the past few moments. Susan's heartbeat, which had been steadily slowing as she rested, now felt as if it were skipping every other beat; she was becoming light-headed. Moving her hand to her breast, she slipped it inside her blouse as if to keep her frightened heart from bursting the confines of her ribcage.

From far away she could hear it coming again, the way it had come one week earlier – the sound of a rushing locomotive. It moved closer and closer, invading the stillness. The sound came from the direction of the forest, a rush of warm air seething through miles of trees, rushing to meet the immovable mass of icy air that, like a fortress, straddled the gateway to the eternity that was the ocean.

The woman grasped her ears and held her breath, just as the furious onslaught collided with the trees nearest the shoreline. They bent and flailed beneath a sky ripped apart in an explosion of thunder that rocked the ground. Then came the inevitable torrent. The sea became a churning cauldron of black turbulence.

Again the sky exploded, pierced through with a shaft of lightning that struck a boulder near the great mound of seaweed out of which she had stolen the body. It sent shivers of granite amid a shower of sparks, then retreated into its cloudy womb.

A stone the size of a man's fist dislodged from the side of the hill and, before the woman could deflect it, came crashing down on the young man. The woman cried out in horror but the sound was swallowed by the screaming wind. Glancing off the young man's face, the rock left a bloodless gash along its cheekbone.

"Oh, Michael, I'm sorry ..." sobbed the woman. She leaned over and kissed the wound. "I've got to get you home. You'll be all right once you're inside."

Looking up at the lighthouse, the hill on which it stood seemed to the woman an insurmountable obstacle, but she soon had an idea.

Quickly removing her overcoat, she wrapped it around the young man's head and tied it securely in place with the coat's belt. Then, grabbing him by the ankles, she began to drag the body up along the rocky path.

Straining at each step, bracing her body against the wind that would have lifted her off the face of the cliff and into the ocean, the woman discovered an unbelievable store of energy as she desperately made her way back to the lighthouse. A few times she almost lost her footing on the slippery stones. But her determination was proving to be a god to her. She noted with satisfaction that although the young man's head continually bounced up and down as it made contact with the black rocks, it was protected by her makeshift wrap.

After what seemed like days, Susan at last stood on the threshold of the lighthouse. Exhausted beyond belief, she mustered her last bit of energy and heaved the body through the doorway, slamming the door against the elements. She let the body drop to the floor of the dimly lit front room, then wearily manoeuvred herself into an old overstuffed chair. Sinking deep into the musty cushions, she stared in the direction of the corpse for several seconds. Its scanty clothing had been torn to shreds by the climb.

Outside, the wind tore at the building and drove mountains of water against the side of the cliff. The woman felt dizzy, imagining the acres of clouds, not far above her, being raked across the sky at 60 miles an hour. A sudden flash of lightning was followed by a flickering of the lights, then a blackout. There was nothing to worry about as far as the beacon was concerned; it would be taken care of by its own generator. She remembered that the shortwave radio was also connected to the independent power source.

For a moment she thought that she should radio the authorities. But, instead, she moved painfully to where the body lay, stretched herself alongside it and fell into a dead sleep.

When she awoke a few hours later, the room was still dark. Through her still closed eyes she noticed a periodic flash, like that of faraway lightning, piercing the night that had fallen over the cape. The second arm of the storm had swept out to sea and all that she could hear now were the waves below. A very faint smell of gas spilled over the floorboards, lacing the steady, cool cross-draft with a vague sense of danger.

Everything seemed hazy to the woman. All that had happened earlier now hovered fitfully at the far edge of her consciousness, with the intensity of something less than a long-forgotten dream and slightly more than utter nonexistence.

She opened her eyes, as if waking to the dark world for the first time, and found herself staring at a cobweb, billowing and subsiding, suspended in the cavernous darkness between the wall and the sofa, appearing and disappearing in the hot flashes of light. She wriggled up and examined it closely.

There, near an extreme limit of the web, a large brown spider was busily feeding astride a massy grey lump of silk. The woman caught her breath for a moment. Ordinarily she would have swept away the cobweb, along with the rest of the dust accumulated in the corners of the floor and ceiling, never bothering to consider the drama of death and survival being played out on the edge of her own mundane existence. A shudder ran the length of her back, and she sat up and rubbed her legs.

She peered into the darkness of the room, trying to collect her thoughts, when her eyes came to rest on the dark figure lying a couple of feet from her. The black waters of her memories burst the reservoir of her subconscious, sending her scrambling forward in its churning wake.

"Oh, Michael ..."

The woman worked vigorously to free the head from its protective cowl. She was amazed at the impossibly tight knots she had managed to tie. When the head was finally free, she let it rest against the wooden floor. The rigor mortis was subsiding and the body was responding more easily. In the harsh white flashes of light, the young man's face seemed to grimace horribly. One of its eyelids had been worked wide-open and the one eye glared accusingly at the woman. This frightened her so much that she began to weep. At that moment, the lights came on again and, when they did, the young man's features seemed to soften in the yellow light.

The woman shifted her weight to her other hand, which came to rest in a small puddle. She pulled back her hand and looked down. A dark-brownish liquid, with the consistency of thin molasses, was seeping out from underneath the body. It was collecting in a little pool in the depression of one of the floorboards. The woman brought her hand to her nose; the odour left no doubt. The body was beginning to putrefy.

She pushed the body over on one side and found the source of the seepage – a series of deep gashes on its back, apparently caused by the journey over the rocks.

"I can't let them find you like this …" she whispered. "I'll have to clean you up first. Then we'll radio them …"

Moments later, she had the young man's body floating peacefully in the gently drawn waters of a warm bath. She sponged his naked flesh with a special cleansing soap.

As he floated in the bath, his willing form submitting to her care without the slightest resistance and she noticed for the first time how beautiful a man he had been. The warm water lent a certain quality to the young man's body, which seemed to mock life. She noted with wonder the strength that must have once resided in the muscular chest, its proud and swelling pectorals responding with exactly the right amount of resilience as she sponged it clean. The young man's thighs and calves had a definition that could only have been carved there, as if in stone, by years of the most painful labour. They were like a pair of sheaths, housing only the most magnificent of swords, she thought, as she meticulously worked the sponge upward, past the wild shock of dark hair framing his manhood, back along the torso, to his face.

"Michael …" she whispered, as she cleansed the nasty gash on his cheek left by the falling rock. She held back tears at the sight of that imperfection in an otherwise perfect figure of beauty. It was as if someone had taken a razor blade to the most exquisite of tapestries.

Her body trembled at the thought of the injustice of it all. She felt offended at nature for having cut off the life of the young man before her, who was himself as flawless a specimen as any human could ever wish to be. His face looked so peaceful, almost radiant, that the woman felt herself suddenly swept up in a rush of exhilaration, a feeling she had never until this very moment felt before.

When she finished drying him, she dressed the wounds on his back. She combed out his long, glossy black hair and dressed him in one of her husband's suits. Then, after laying him face up on the long glass table in the front room, she sat cross-legged on the floor opposite him.

She felt that it was now time she radio the police but another force was simultaneously working on her. Something still seemed unfinished.

As she sat there, gazing at the young man, his long hair flowing over the edge of the table, swaying in the cross draft, an odd thought struck her. She knew that when they came, they would take him away. They would humiliate him by stripping him naked and shoving him into an ice cold drawer at the morgue, until he could be identified. But what if he wasn't identified; what if nobody came to claim him?

"No! I won't let them take you ..."

She moved to the young man's side and looked down at his striking features. Her fingers traced a delicate path over his eyelids, his nose, his lips. She tried to imagine what he would want her to do. Moving to her knees, she brought her face close to his. She took in the pleasant scent of bath oil. It reminded her of the camellias that blossomed in her mother's garden, the way they breathed their perfume into the sultry air of a summer evening. She was pleased that the young man could share the experience of this memory with her. She moved her ear ever so close to his lips to hear what he would have her do.

He seemed to whisper something unintelligible to her, in a voice as quiet as his breathing. The woman moved her ear even closer until it was pressed hard against the young man's mouth. Then she heard the words again: *Bury me ...*

—⚌—

Grinding its way through the mud, a large state jeep approached the lighthouse through the woods. Its bright headlights reflected off the drizzling rain, making it difficult for Sheriff Glen Peterson and his passenger, Susan's husband, Richard Fultz, to see very far down the road.

Sheriff Peterson felt odd whenever he had to come to the lighthouse. Each time he saw it, he was reminded of his boyhood on the coast of northern New England, where lighthouses were a familiar sight. Something about the way they looked, always standing alone, struck a melancholy note in the man.

Over the years, the lighthouse had come to symbolise, for Sheriff Peterson, all the solitude in the world. He had often found himself fighting against the desire to turn his eyes away from these buildings. And yet, at the same time, he was aware of an undeniable compulsion to be in the presence of the eternally revolving beacon, glaring into the face of a starless night shrouding the bottomless ocean. This was why he had so readily agreed to drive his old friend Richard over the washed-out road leading through the forest to the promontory. It was the perfect excuse to come out and see the lighthouse in its perfect element – a storm.

As the vehicle rolled to a stop in front of the building, they could see that it was dark inside. Except for the revolving beacon, the only light visible was a very faint flickering in the front room. Sheriff Peterson looked over at Richard, who sat quietly in his seat. His silence was in sharp contrast to his usual talkative, carefree self.

"What's the matter?" asked Sheriff Peterson.

Richard returned his look; his face clouded over. "I don't know ... but something's definitely up."

Sheriff Peterson studied his friend's face. He had always hated his secretiveness. It had become more acute since he had taken the job as lighthouse keeper five years ago, and even worse since he had married a year later. At first, like any good friend who feels his place has been usurped, he had blamed Richard's increasing aloofness on Susan, Richard's wife.

She was nice enough whenever he had come out to visit, but quiet, very quiet. Once Richard and he had settled into a conversation, she would always break away and sit with her back turned to them, staring, always staring with those icy grey eyes of hers, out of the window at the ocean. He had interpreted her quietness as a sign that he wasn't welcome and eventually he stopped coming altogether, except for his official biannual visits.

"Maybe she's asleep," he suggested.

"Maybe so ..."

"So, let's check it out," said Sheriff Peterson, opening the car door.

"Say, Glen ... you wouldn't mind waiting here, would you?"

Just as I expected, thought the sheriff.

"Here?"

"Yeah, just for a second."

The sheriff tried to suppress a feeling of disappointment. He didn't understand why at his age he could still feel hurt by the seemingly innocuous words of a friend. He swallowed hard.

"Why?"

"It's Susan ... You know, she's been nervous lately. She might get alarmed if she sees me with you at this time of night," said Richard, sitting there as if waiting for an answer.

Sheriff Peterson was glad his friend hadn't simply stepped out of the car. "How long were you away this time?" he asked.

"Almost two weeks."

Peterson shook his head.

Richard hopped out of the Jeep, stepped up to the building and peered through one of its small windows. He could make out the form of someone sitting in the middle of the front room, on the floor.

Circling round to another window, he strained to get a clearer view. From this vantage point, he recognised that the form was his wife. She was kneeling in the middle of the room, wearing one of her seldom-worn formal dresses, her eyes fixed on something in front of her that he couldn't quite see. Something went tight in Richard's chest. He moved back around the building to the front door and let himself in. Stepping through the entryway, he turned the corner into the front room.

"Susan, are you all right –?" He caught his breath at the sight before him.

Susan turned her head away from the man who was lying on the coffee table – two candles at his head, two at his feet – and appeared to look past her husband. Her dull eyes glistened sickeningly in the candlelight.

"What's going on here …?" whispered Richard.

"I found him," she said, in a dreadful monotone. "He washed up on the beach during the storm."

Richard stared at his wife, half in disbelief, half in fear. He had known she was becoming increasingly unbalanced, especially over the past few months. But for reasons that were still a mystery to him, it gave him a certain pleasure not to care.

He knew that she hated to be left alone; he also knew that she didn't have the strength to do anything to change her situation. She was the perfect, submissive wife. This, however, took him by complete surprise. Her steel-grey eyes appeared to be looking into his soul. They seemed to know his thoughts.

"Why did you leave me alone?" she asked dully.

"I, uh … you know, I had to go up to Portland on some business," he said, staring at the corpse. "The storm … it kept me away. It washed out the road. I was lucky enough to convince Glen Peterson to four-wheel me in."

Susan's face darkened at the mention of the name. "Sheriff Peterson? Is he here?" she asked.

"Right outside."

There was a long pause, with neither husband nor wife knowing what to say next. Outside, the wind was picking up speed once again. It forcefully blew open the front door, shaking the building and causing the flames of the candles to sputter. Richard and Susan continued to stare at each other.

"Richard …?" said Susan, finally breaking the silence.

"What?"

"Can I ask you something?"

Richard nodded.

"Why did you bring me here in the first place?"

"Oh, for Christ's sake, Susan! There's a dead guy lying on our coffee table, dressed in my clothes!"

Richard rushed at his wife, who put up her hands to fend him off. He grabbed her by the shoulders and she began to sob. "I didn't want to leave him on the beach!" she screamed.

"Goddamn you …" he said, shaking her violently.

"Stop it!" she cried, trying to pull herself loose.

He let go of her, sending her sprawling to the floor.

"Did you even think to radio the Coast Guard?" he asked.

"Yes … I thought about it," she answered, sitting up and pulling aside the hair that had fallen in her face.

"And, did you?"

"No."

"Go! Do it now."

Susan slid across the floor in the direction of the corpse. "I'm not leaving him," she said.

"Susan, I'm warning you. I want you to go into the radio room this very second and call the Coast Guard. Tell them what you found."

"Why don't you ask your good buddy Sheriff Peterson to come inside."

"Glen is not going to see this. Go and radio the Coast Guard. Go!"

Susan got up from the floor and moved timidly toward the winding staircase.

At that moment, Sheriff Peterson stuck his head through the open doorway. "Say, what's going on in ... Jesus H Christ! What the hell is that?"

"Oh, Christ ..." said Richard, shaking his head. "Susan found this guy washed up on the beach."

"His name's Michael ..." whispered Susan, stepping back into the room.

"Now, how in the hell do you know that?" asked Richard.

Susan held out her hand, from which dangled the little gold chain.

Richard and his friend exchanged glances. The sheriff took the chain from Susan's hand.

"You're going to take him away, aren't you?"

"Just shut up, Susan! Not one more word."

"Easy there, Rich," said the sheriff, laying his hand on his friend's shoulder. He turned to Susan. "Yes, I'm afraid I'll have to take the body back with me."

"I thought so ..." she said, then moved to a corner of the room and sat down.

"Hey, Rich," said the sheriff in a lowered voice, "can I use your radio for a minute?"

"I'd rather you use the radio in your Jeep, if it's all the same," said Richard.

The sheriff glanced at Susan, then back at Richard. "Sure you're OK to stay here?"

"Yes, for god's sake," said Richard, "I'll deal with this. You go do what you have to do."

Sheriff Peterson raised his hands in surrender and beat a hasty retreat.

Richard fidgeted with his key chain, looking at his wife as she sat cowering in the corner. He wondered why he had reacted so angrily toward her. Certainly it wasn't her fault that she had found the body. But why had she lavished such attention on it? Why hadn't she radioed the authorities? He moved to take a closer look at the corpse.

Scanning the body with the intensity of a jealous lover, he caught his breath. There, very near the young man's mouth, on the cheek facing the far wall, was a smudge of dark red lipstick, the same colour his wife was wearing.

"Susan!" he called. His voice echoed through the building, spiralling up the staircase. It seemed to catch in the cold draft that was sweeping across the room, causing the candles to sputter.

Richard watched as the flames leaned dangerously in the direction of the young man's head. He stood there for a moment, half expecting, half hoping to see the dead man's long hair burst into flames – a blazing halo – when he heard a shuffling at his back. He turned and found his wife standing behind him, one hand covering her mouth, barely breathing. She brushed past him and sat next to the coffee table once again.

"Susan ..." he said, moving in her direction. "Did you ... did you know this guy?"

Richard regarded his wife, sitting on the floor in what seemed to be a trance and, for the first time in months, felt a desire to be close to her, to comfort her. He wondered where this desire was coming from, whether it was some vestige of the ardour he had once felt for her long ago, or just a form of guilt at having shirked his husbandly duties. Either way, he knew her present condition was partly his fault, arising from some neglect and from having left her alone so often whilst he went off on his "business trips". The rest of tonight would belong to her, he resolved. He felt it was the least he could do, considering how difficult tomorrow would be. He didn't think she would hold up well to the questions that would be put to her. The thought brought back the unpleasantness, and the instinct to fix the blame for the whole incident on her arose once again, but he fought it back.

Moving to where she was sitting, Richard lowered himself to the floor next to his wife.

"Susan ... how about if we go on upstairs," he said, warmly placing his hand on her shoulder. Her body went rigid. "Come on, Susan, it's all over now. Why don't you relax a bit, then go to bed."

"What will they do with him?" she asked, her voice barely audible.

Richard looked askance at his wife, then let go of her. Disgust welled up inside of him again. He stood and moved to the kitchen.

"I'm going to make a pot of coffee. You want some?" he asked.

Susan shook her head in response as she got to her feet and started out of the room.

"Where are you going?" asked her husband.

"Upstairs ..." she answered, "I'm tired."

"Want me to come up with you?"

Susan never answered, but only crept up the spiral staircase.

Richard stared out of the kitchen window into the darkness shrouding the cape. There was no moon, no stars. Every 15 seconds the beacon would make its circuit, illuminating for a moment the waves crashing on the rocks below, a lone freighter in the distance, a narrow band of phosphorescence, all to be consumed once again by another 15 seconds of darkness. Very soon the sun would be rising in another attempt to assault the cover of clouds. Perhaps this time it would succeed.

As he drained the last bit of coffee from the Styrofoam cup, Richard thought of the woman upstairs. He had hoped that she would be the answer to his loneliness. Instead, his years with her had taught him the full meaning of loneliness, a loneliness from which he had sought to escape, a loneliness from which he would never find relief.

Lost in thought, he moved away from the window. Susan would probably still be lying awake in bed, staring stupidly at the ceiling, he thought. Absently crushing the coffee cup in his hand, he let it fall from his fingers to the floor as he trudged up the winding staircase.

The Shovelist

Guillaume Morin stood at his kitchen window, peering through the falling snow. Across the street, two men in matching brown leather jackets were unloading boxes from a metallic blue Cadillac and lugging them into Suzanne Sillery's old place.

"Stop staring! It's not proper."

Guillaume looked at his wife. She was seated at the kitchen table, pretending to focus on her daily crossword puzzle, but he knew she was as curious about Magog's newest arrivals as he was. Anne made it her business to know everyone else's.

"Diane Lapointe heard from the estate agent that they're Pakistanis from Toronto," she added.

"They don't look like Pakistanis to me," said Guillaume.

Anne set down the newspaper and glared at him over the rim of her glasses. "When was the last time you saw a Pakistani?"

Guillaume shrugged and looked back out of the window. "What do you suppose they're doing here?"

"Don't know and don't care," she said, carefully writing a word into the puzzle. "I don't much like the look of the pair of them."

Guillaume poured himself a steaming mug of coffee and shuffled to the kitchen table.

"They look fine to me," he murmured.

Anne set down the newspaper. "All I know is you'd better make sure they let you shovel their snow," she said. "Because if it's shovelry they need, you're the one to do it."

"That's not a word."

"What isn't?"

"Shovelry. It's not a proper word." Guillaume glanced at the crossword puzzle. "And neither is this," he added, pointing at the grid.

"Ha!" Guillaume's wife said, swatting away his hand. "Another English lesson from Professor Over-the-Hill."

Guillaume smiled, drained the last of the coffee from his mug, and stood tall. "In any case," he said, "my arrangement was with Suzanne, not with them."

"Maybe she told them about your arrangement."

Guillaume stretched his weary legs and returned to the window in time to see the young men haul the last few boxes on their porch and into the house. As he contemplated the pair, he vaguely wondered, not for the first time since he'd retired, just when did he and Anne get so old? Was it that long ago that they were moving into their own house as newlyweds? He had returned home early from the war, having suffered a major shrapnel wound. Fifty years later his hip still pained him, especially on cold days like this.

"Go introduce yourself," Anne's voice cut into his musing.

Guillaume narrowed his eyes at his wife. "Don't you think we should at least let them settle in before we bother them?"

"Bother them? Guillaume Morin, you get yourself over there this second and don't come back until they've agreed to let you shovel. We can't afford to lose that money. Not with that miserable pension of yours."

Knowing she was right, Guillaume sighed, pulled on his parka and homespun cap, and hobbled to the door. "Too old for this," he mumbled as he stepped outside and braced himself against the penetrating cold wind. "A man ought to be someplace warm like Florida."

He slogged across the snow-choked road until he reached the shining Cadillac, trying his best to look casual, hoping the young men might come out of the house again and save him the trouble of knocking on their door.

"What are you doing?" his wife shouted from the doorway. "Knock on the door!" She balled her hand into a fist and made a pantomime of pounding the air.

Guillaume waved her off and grumbled as he moved cautiously up the steps to the icy porch. Just as he lifted the brass knocker, the front door flew open and Guillaume found himself facing one of the young men. The knocker landed with a ringing *thwack*! – startling them both. The young man appeared to be in his 30s, wore his blue-black hair closely cropped and sported a smartly groomed goatee.

"Um, hello," he said, staring curiously at Guillaume. "Can I help you?"

The other man stuck his head out the door. He was obviously much younger, clean-shaven with large, almond-shaped eyes. "Who's this?" he said.

Guillaume attempted a smile but already his face felt frozen solid. He gestured across the street and managed the word "neighbour".

"What was that?" the younger of the two said.

"He said 'neighbour'," said the other. "Is that right, sir? You're our neighbour?"

Guillaume nodded. He regretted having crossed the street. Meeting new people, he reminded himself, was not his strong point. Fortunately, he thought, new people rarely appeared in this part of the Eastern Townships, least of all Pakistanis from Toronto.

"It's freezing," the man with the goatee said, moving back into the house. "Would you like to come inside?"

Firing a backward glance across the street to see his wife still standing in the doorway, Guillaume nodded and crossed the threshold into Suzanne Sillery's former home. The young men ushered him through a maze of boxes, bags and suitcases into the living room. Guillaume looked around but didn't see anywhere to sit.

"I'm Jake Abulafia," the goateed man said. "This is my boyfriend, Ronny Dwek." He thrust his hand toward Guillaume. "And you are …?"

"I'm the shovelist," Guillaume replied, shaking the proffered hand.

The two young men exchanged a glance.

"I'm sorry," Ronny said, raising an eyebrow at Jake, "you're the what?"

"The shovelist. I do the shovelling. For the snow."

"What do you mean?" Jake said. "They have snowploughs here, I'm sure."

Guillaume shook his head. "For the streets, yes, of course, but I'm the shovelist for this house – front porch, side yard, backyard, deck."

"I'm going to make some tea," Ronny said with a curt shake of his head. "Would you like some?" He moved to the kitchen without waiting for an answer.

"We've always shovelled our own snow actually," Jake said. "Thank you anyway."

"But," Guillaume reddened a bit and he cast his eyes about the room for a moment, wondering what would happen to his own house when he and Anne were gone. He had heard that Suzanne's children had sold most of her beautiful furniture and all her paintings, clearly more interested in the cash than keeping what their mother had worked so hard to acquire. Now, nothing of substance remained. Only the shell of a house filled with boxes belonging to new owners. Who would move into his house when he was gone, he wondered. Someone from the townships? Or strangers?

Guillaume was suddenly aware that Jake was staring at him. He coughed into his glove and wiped it on the seat of his trousers. "I always shovelled for Madame Sillery. The woman who lived here before you," he said, looking at the empty walls. "She painted," he added.

"Did she?" Jake said distractedly, wondering where Ronny had got to with the tea. "You know, we have quite a lot to do at the moment." He pointed at the unopened boxes. "Perhaps we might speak about this again, some other time. But stay for a cup of tea first. It's dreadful out there today. We're not used to seeing this much snow."

Guillaume stared hard at the floor, praying for a solution to this dilemma. He didn't want to explain to his wife that he had lost the contract. She would blame him throughout the long winter for not selling himself hard enough. He could imagine her nattering at him all day, all night, that if someone needed shovelry, then he was the best man around and it was all a matter of his convincing these young men.

"Well," he answered, his legs stiffening from standing so long in one position, "I don't guess you get much snow in Pakistan."

Ronny was just walking into the living room carrying a brass serving tray on which he balanced three teacups, a teapot and a creamer. He cocked his head and stared strangely at the old man. "Pakistan?"

—ɯ—

"Did you get it?" Guillaume's wife said, as he hung his parka on one of the coat pegs.

Guillaume pulled off his mittens with his teeth, hobbled over to the blazing fireplace and held up his hands against the warmth.

His wife crossed her arms and glared at him.

"They're not Pakistanis," Guillaume said, staring into the flames.

"What?" The woman took a step toward Guillaume.

"Remember, I told you they didn't look like Pakistanis, and you said, how would I know?" he said, half-turning to peer at his wife out of the corner of his eye. "Well I was right. They're not. They're some kind of Jewish or Spanish. Work for the government."

She rolled her eyes at him. "I don't care where they're from. Did you get the contract or didn't you?"

"Yes, Anne, I got it," Guillaume muttered. He creaked toward the bedroom before stopping to turn back to his wife, touching her cheek. "Don't worry, poppet. We'll be all right."

—⁘—

"What's that noise?"

Jake rolled over in bed and opened one eye. Ronny was sitting bolt upright, his hair sticking up like a black jaggedy cockscomb.

"What noise?"

Ronny raised a finger and cocked his head. A moment later, a faint scrape-scrape-scraping sound floated into the room. Ronny instantly leapt out of bed, flung back the blinds and looked outside.

"That crazy old man's shovelling our driveway."

He rapped on the window several times, then turned to Jake, a look of exasperation on his face. "He's ignoring me."

Jake glanced at the clock on his nightstand and shook his head. "I'm sure he can't hear you. It's 6.30 in the morning, for fuck's sake, Ronny, go back to sleep."

"But you told him no," Ronny said, looking back outside at the old man, who was moving slowly to the side yard, the shovel trailing behind him leaving an impotent rut in the snow.

"I'll talk to him later." Jake fluffed his pillow and pulled it over his face. "Come back to bed," came his muffled voice.

Ronny quickly padded around to Jake's side of the bed and yanked the pillow off his head.

"You're not going to let him shovel after you told him not to, are you?"

"Why not?" Jake said, prying the pillow from Ronny's grip.

"Because it's not right! People can't just go doing whatever they want on other people's properties because they feel like it."

"Maybe he thought I said he could do our shovelling."

Ronny marched to the closet, extracted Jake's bathrobe, and held it out to him. "Go tell him to stop."

Jake sat up and rubbed his face. "I have an idea," he said, "Let's just let him do our shovelling today. It'll save us the time and trouble and will likely do the old guy some good, too."

Ronny let the bathrobe drop to the floor and stormed out of the room. He raced down the stairs to the sliding glass door at the back of the house. Guillaume was starting to clear the snow from the steps leading up to the back deck. Ronny knocked vigorously on the glass door and Guillaume looked up at him, lifting a mittened hand in a weak attempt at a wave. Ronny signalled him over to the door.

"Good morning," Guillaume said, his breath billowing through the narrow opening. "It's a cold one today."

Ronny looked at the shovel then back up at the old man. He looked somehow different in the blue light of early morning. He could see that the old man had been once handsome in his youth, but his face was now deeply lined and chapped an angry red. A rheumy film was starting to cover the iris of his left eye, and his right eye was shot through with spidery veins. The lanky old man would have stood over six feet tall if it were not for a noticeable stoop, a sagging of the head as if his neck could no longer support its weight. Despite his posture, the old man carried himself with a clear sense of dignity.

"You're shovelling our snow," Ronny said quietly.

The old man nodded, "I'm the best shovelist around."

"But we told you not to."

Guillaume looked down at his boots for a moment, then looked back up at Ronny and pulled himself to his full height, clearing his throat. "This is a sample of my work. For free, of course – to see if you like it. You can let me know tomorrow if you're pleased with the job." He continued to shovel, as though the matter were settled.

—〰—

Some time later, Jake came downstairs in his bathrobe and stockinged feet to find Ronny sitting on a box in the living room, staring thoughtfully into a cup of Earl Grey. "I was beginning to wonder what happened to you," he said.

Ronny took a considered sip, then rose from the box to make his way into the kitchen. "We're going to have to go out for breakfast," he called over his back. "All the cooking stuff is still packed away."

"Right," Jake said, following him, "but what about the old man? Did you talk to him?"

"I did," Ronny said, staring out at the back deck, now completely cleared of snow. "I told him it was all right. He can do our shovelling."

"You're kidding."

"Like you said," Ronny put the tea kettle on the stove, "it will save us the trouble, and will be good for Guillaume."

"Who?"

"Guillaume. His name is Guillaume Morin. I realised while I was outside that we never got his name yesterday."

Jake looked out of the window. The removal of the snow was irregular at best: perfect in some spots, downright sloppy in others. He looked back at Ronny, a doubtful expression on his face.

"Guillaume?"

"Guillaume, and Anne, his wife. You know, it's not a bad job for an old guy."

Jake looked out the window again, then shook his head and moved to the kitchen to pour some boiling water into the teapot.

"We can always fix it later," Ronny added. "It's not a big deal."

Jake opened his mouth, calculating a clever retort, when he caught sight of Guillaume out their front window, his shovel slung over his shoulder, striding across the road toward his house. He looked back at Ronny with a slight shrug of his shoulders. "I guess we should finish unpacking these fucking boxes."

Tiger at Beaufort Point

"Tiger by the river! Tiger by the river!"
    Screams and shouts and laughter and the whoooosh of my neighbours rushing past our house drew me outside and on to the front porch. My little sister, Sylvie, disengaged from the mad rush of people and ran up to me, red-faced and huffapuffing.

"Jean-Jacques, hurry! A big tiger ..." She grabbed me by the arm with her strong tiny hands, dragged me into the crowd and I ran with them – skipping and tripping and flibbertigibbetting over poodles and schmoodles, toddlers and tricycles, and any-thing else that was unlucky enough to get in my way.

"What ho!" my mother screamed, waving peanut-butter-and-jelly sandwiches at us from the front door. "Where you going, you two?" Her screams faded into the background as we rounded the corner and charged up Main Street toward the village centre.

All week long, the town's gossipmongers circulated the incredible rumour that a tiger was coming to town. No one really believed it. And yet, here we were, the whole town, stam-peding like a herd of buffalo toward what we hoped was an actual real live tiger – my favourite animal of all time.

"Where's this tiger, eh?" old man Papineau yelled from his electric wheelchair as it buzzed down the sidewalk.

"The river, the river!" shrieked Fat Suzanne Sillery, strong-arming her way past me. "They're shooting a movie down there."

The word MOVIE electrified the crowd like a cattle prod in the bum and, before I knew it, some unidentified- running-lardo had knocked me to the ground. Curling up like a pill bug, I tried my best not to get squished by the scores of feet stamping all around me.

When the last pair of hairy legs ran by, I stuck up my head –
covering my nose and mouth against a big cloud of dust – and
watched, out of breath, as the mob swept past the Chateau Bleu
on its way over the bridge that spans the Magog river.

"You OK?"

I whirled around and found Sheriff Hebert's tomboy daughter, Chantal, standing over me, her hand extended in my
direction. Chantal's father had been transferred to our town
from Montreal a few months ago and, as far as I knew, they both
hated it here. I grabbed hold of Chantal's hand and she yanked
me to my feet.

"Thanks," I said, brushing myself off.

"Those people are insane," she said, shaking her head.

"There's a tiger ..." I pointed toward the river.

"Yeah, I know all about it. It's from Gil Poulin's Exotic
Menagerie. He's walking the damned thing through town,
trying to get it used to being around people and cars and stuff.
For a Hollywood movie, he says."

"You don't want to see it?"

"It's a tiger, you know," Chantal said, cutting her eyes at me.

"Yeah, so?"

"It ain't in a cage."

"It's not walking around loose, is it?"

Chantal shrugged. "Probably not."

"Well, I'm not going to miss out," I said, starting down the
sidewalk, "Tigers are my absolute all-time favourite animal."

"Hold up!" She jogged over to me and grabbed my shoulder.
"My dad told me he's going to shoot it."

The breath went out of me as if Chantal had slugged me in
the stomach. Her father was a mean bastard and, if he said he'd
shoot the tiger, I knew he would.

"He warned Poulin not to bring it around here," Chantal
said, "but Poulin's crazy. Said it was his right to walk it wherever
he wanted."

"If he's got it on a leash it's probably OK." The saliva had all but evaporated from my mouth. "Besides, your father can't just go firing off a gun around all those people."

Chantal stared in the direction of the bridge. "Listen to me," she said after a moment, "you'd better not go – really. My dad says anyone idiot enough to get up close to an uncaged tiger deserves to get shot, too."

"That's totally stupid!" I shook free of her hand and started off down the road.

"All right, go see your tiger, you stupid bumpkin," Chantal shouted. "Just remember to hang back and stand clear, if you know what's good for you."

I mounted the bridge and raced toward Beaufort Point and the river's edge – to warn Poulin and to see the tiger.

And just there, dead ahead and to the left of the railroad tracks, it seemed the entire town was assembled near the water. I couldn't see anything yet except the mass of people, a couple of thousand strong, and three squad cars.

Reaching the edge of the crowd, I pushed into it, determined to make it to the front. I dropped to my knees where the crowd was thickest and crawled between their legs.

Breathing was difficult in the suffocating, stifling heat of so many bodies pressed together. I imagined I was pushing through a dense forest, no, a jungle … and on the other side of that jungle I would find a tiger.

After a few mad minutes I saw light ahead, a clearing. I crawled and pushed and clawed my way the last few feet until, at last, I emerged and found myself drawing big gulps of fresh air at the water's edge.

And there it was …

Big tiger by the river. Powerful. Huge. A massive, beautiful cat. Orange sherbet with chocolate swirls. Flash of emeralds for eyes. Yellow-green, opalescent. And I hang back. I stand clear.

Screams and shouts and laughter.

Nervous, cagey, pacing side to side at the end of a leash, choke collar around its neck. Light years from easy. And Sheriff Hebert watching from atop a rocky knoll. And those eyes ...

Hang back – stand clear, I want to scream, but the tiger's gaze silences me.

Unaccustomed to so many humans gawking and pointing at it, something inside the tiger rumbles. And I hang back. I stand clear.

An imbecile reaches out, offers it a mustard-smeared pretzel. Another dangles a slab of jerky toward it. "Here, kitty kitty kitty. Here, kitty kitty."

Screams and shouts and laughter.

Something inside the tiger, inside of me, goes tight – pushes some back, pulls some forward. All the while, I hang back. I stand clear.

Tiger-tiger catches sight out of the corner of its glistening eye – waving hands; junk-food offerings – lunges at the crowd, pulls taut the leash in Poulin's hand. Crowd screams. Fear replaces laughter.

Instant of rope burn and then a choke ... and a choke ... the tiger breaks free. Takes a swipe at a group of school kids.

A gunshot and the simultaneous yelp of the tiger splits the air. Then – the orange-black body slumps heavy to the ground. Now forever still.

I watch in horror as a stream of blood flows from the tiger's head down the embankment and into the river. Light fades from its startled, open eyes.

Two thousand people stand silent, stunned – for a moment. Then they drift away. Everyone except Poulin (cradling the tiger's head in his trembling hands), Sheriff Hebert (ordering Poulin to step away from the carcass NOW) and me (on my knees and tearing up fistfuls of grass).

Years would pass before I dared chase after tigers again.

Cactuses

Two saguaro cactuses sat snugly in one of the Berliner's many clay pots. He smiled to see the larger of the two had already blossomed. Its single pink flower, perched above a network of thorns, seemed to quiver from some internal wind. The young man standing beside him reached out a finger.

"No, don't." The Berliner intercepted the young man's finger with a quick snatch of his hand. "It doesn't like to be touched."

The young man disengaged his finger from the old man's grasp and frowned at him. "It won't hurt, Mr Eisenwahr. They're sturdy enough plants."

The old man cast a glance at his visitor, who returned his look with an air of boredom. "Why hasn't the other one bloomed?" Eisenwahr asked.

"How would I know?" the young man snapped.

"You seem to be the type that would know."

"The type? What type is that?"

"One of these south-western types, Mexican or perhaps Native American?"

"My parents are Cuban."

"Cuban, is that so?" Eisenwahr looked genuinely astonished. "Isn't that curious? That a Cuban and a German should meet in Southern California ..."

"What's so curious about that? I'm sure you've met with stranger pairings, considering all the places you've lived in your obviously long life." The young man stared at the prickly man and narrowed his eyes at him for a moment. "How old are you, anyway?"

A smile played on Eisenwahr's lips as he studied the young man standing before him. He found his arrogance attractive. After entertaining scores of visitors, who were always so awestruck to be in his presence, he found this young egoist refreshing.

"How old do you think I am?"

The young man stepped back and stared at the Berliner. All the photographs and drawings he had seen of the writer had been composed much earlier in his life. His once handsome face was now drawn and angular. His thick blond hair was now totally replaced with wisps of grey.

"I have no idea. I guess, maybe 75."

"Eighty one." Eisenwahr took the young man by the hand. "Come inside, I've got something to show you – a surprise."

"Another one?"

The young man allowed himself to be pulled along, turning his head once to look back at the cactuses.

Eisenwahr led him through his spacious estate overlooking the Pacific Ocean, built on the border separating Santa Monica from the Palisades. They padded down a hallway that led into a vast living room.

"Look at this," the old man said, moving to the picture window, "a magnificent view, is it not?"

"Why don't you live in Malibu?"

"I feel safer up here. I'm in no danger of being swept out to sea."

"True, I guess." The young man strolled over to the bookcase. "Until the big one shakes us all to hell." He picked out a copy of the Bhagavad Gita and examined it closely. A heady smell of patchouli permeated the air. "You got this place all to yourself?"

Eisenwahr moved to the young man's side and snatched the book out of his hand, replacing it on the bookshelf. "No, I have a companion who lives with me."

"Oh yeah? Where is he?"

"He's away. Come with me into my study. We'll be more comfortable there."

When they arrived at the study, Eisenwahr let go of the young man's hand and moved to the back of the room. He leaned heavily on the bureau behind him.

"You all right?" the young man asked.

"No, I'm not all right." Eisenwahr stared hard at the young man. "I'm going to die soon."

"Why is that?" he said, narrowing his eyes at the old man. "Are you sick?"

"Not particularly. At least not physically."

"So how could you possibly know?"

"I just know. Death and I," he said quietly, "we are well acquainted."

"Sorry to hear that." The young man suppressed a yawn with the back of his hand.

The ticking of a windup clock on the bureau cut through the silence that followed. The young man stared at it for a moment, then looked back at the Berliner and raised his thick eyebrows expectantly. "I don't have all day, you know."

"I see," Eisenwahr said. "Well, to the point then. Mr Rider tells me you fancy yourself a writer."

"Yeah, Rider's a nice guy," the young man said with a smirk. "He said you might be able to help me."

"Perhaps. What is it exactly you would like me to do for you?"

"Read my work, I guess. Maybe make a few suggestions."

"Is that what you have in your hand?" Eisenwahr pointed at the large manila envelope the young man held limply at his side.

"Huh? Oh yeah. Do you want to read it now? It's a short story called *Invitation to the Dominant Culture*."

"What an intriguing title," Eisenwahr said. "Place it there on the desk, I'll get to it later."

The young man shrugged, tossed the envelope atop the bureau and unbuttoned the top two buttons of his shirt. He looked up at the Berliner.

"What are you staring at?" Eisenwahr said.

"You don't look very well."

The Berliner was starting to resent his guest's lack of enthusiasm. "Young man, do you have any idea who I am?"

"Of course I do."

"Tell me," Eisenwahr said.

"You're Kristian Eisenwahr," the young man said. "Rider tells me you were a great writer back in the day."

A troubled expression spread over Eisenwahr's deeply lined face. When the old man spoke again, his voice was quieter: "Kristian Eisenwahr was born on a farm. He was of peasant stock. Great writers don't come from such humble origins."

"I wouldn't know," the young man said. He slipped off his shirt and placed it on the bureau.

An intense expression of dissatisfaction rippled across the old man's face, the way the surface of a mirror warps when exposed to an intense heat. Then, with a sudden burst of energy, he strode to the centre of the room, raised his arms to the ceiling and cried out: "I am Kristian Eisenwahr, goddamn you all." He cast his eyes about the room. "I plough the fields of ardour with indigo, graphite and blood!" He levelled his gaze at the young man. "Do you know who you are," he asked, pointing a crooked finger at him, "you pathetic creature?"

The young man backed away in shock.

"Answer me," Eisenwahr said.

"I've got to get going …"

The young man gabbed his shirt and started for the door, but he was intercepted by Eisenwahr, who took him by the arm and held him fast.

"I'll tell you who you are," he said, pressing his dry lips against the young man's ear and hissing, "you're nothing."

The young man shook off Eisenwahr's grip. "I'm nothing?" he said, backing away from him. "Well, I guess that beats being a disgusting old man."

"I may be a disgusting old man, as you say, but I'm a disgusting old man who has made it. You're just disgusting," he said. "And you're arrogant, too. That's a poor combination for an aspiring author."

"I see ..."

"Don't misunderstand me, please. I think you're a very attractive young man. It's your attitude that needs improvement."

The young man blinked at Eisenwahr, then shook his head.

"What is it?" Eisenwahr said.

"This is really fucked up."

"I forbid you to use that kind of language in my presence. There is so much you could learn from me; you have no idea. How dare you disrespect me."

The young man held up his hands. "All right, all right! I'm sorry, OK?" He took a step backward and felt the closed door behind him. "Just stop getting all crazy on me."

Eisenwahr nodded at the young man. He was pleased with the apology. He took a step toward him. "Look at me," he said. "I've devoted my entire life to art. But art is passive and artificial. It's nothing. This, however," he said, running a cold finger down the young man's chest, "this is reality."

The young man closed his eyes and shook his head. "Maybe your art is nothing," he said, "but I've seen some damned beautiful art."

"Come now, young man, enough with the philosophising." The Berliner took a final step forward, closing the gap between them. His voice took an intimate tone.

"The truth of the matter is," he said, "we artists have turned our backs on reality." He took the young man by the arm and led him to a couch at the opposite end of the room. "We dream for others, but never really do anything ourselves." He flipped a switch on the stereo and the first strains of a Wagnerian opera filled the room. "Action ..." he said, locking the door to his study. "Action is where you'll find true beauty," he said, flashing a row of yellow teeth.

—⟋⟍—

Half an hour later, the door to Eisenwahr's study opened and out stepped the young man, alone.

"Can you find your way to the door?" called the voice of the Berliner.

The young man didn't answer. His face was devoid of expression. Moving down the hall, he soon reached the front door and stepped out into the bright afternoon.

He stood on the steps of the house for a moment, waiting for his eyes to adjust to the light, when he noticed the clay pot he had seen earlier. Drawing a breath, he reached out his hand and fingered the pink flower. Then, with a quick backward glance, he plucked the flower off the cactus and crushed it in his hand. Hurrying down the driveway to the street, he let its remains fall to the pavement.

He rounded the corner at the bottom of the hill and approached his girlfriend's Karmann Ghia. She was waiting inside, listening to the radio. The young man opened the passenger door and sat next to her. He reached into the glove box, pulled out a pair of sunglasses and slipped them on. His girlfriend wrinkled her brow at him as he sat low in his seat.

"Well?" she said, after a moment.

"Well what?" He stared straight ahead at the sun as it dipped into the Pacific.

"Did he like your work?"

"I don't know ..."

"You don't know? What did he say?"

"Nothing much."

"He must have said something. My God, you were in there long enough!"

The young man reached over and snapped off the radio. "He said he was dying."

"Oh ..."

Both of them remained silent for a few moments. Outside, the cicadas were just taking up their cry. The young man's girl-friend reached out her hand and laid it on his shoulder.

He looked at her out of the corner of his sunglasses then, raising himself in his seat, rolled down his window and spat on the road.

"C'mon," he muttered, "let's get the hell out of here."

Invitation to the Dominant Culture

The first time I read *Portnoy's Complaint*, I was barely 12 years old. I found it quite by accident, wrongly shelved in the children's reading room of our public library. After leafing through the first few pages, I decided to become better acquainted with it, so I took it into the toilet.

Now, so you're not disappointed later on, let me tell you right upfront – this is not going to be another whack-off story à la Philip Roth. Also, I'm not Jewish and I'm not into psychoanalysis – although my parents sent me to a psychiatrist once because I thought I was Jewish (for a very good reason, which will become apparent in due course). I'm only using this little reminiscence to illustrate a point. I'm convinced whatever intelligent force pulls the strings of the universe out there has a rather odd sense of humor.

What I mean to say is no matter how hard my parents tried to shelter me from the "corrupting influences of the dominant culture," they found their way to me anyway. Like that book.

I'm sure they meant well, these incurably Catholic parents of mine. Who, after all, wouldn't want to have Saint Francis as a son? But the 18 years I spent under their influence – including the nine years of Catholic elementary and junior high school and the four years I spent in seminary (a fancy name for an all-boys high school) – did things to my mind beyond my parents' holiest fantasies, things that leave me cold and confused, shaking my fist at the empty sky and asking:

How did I get here? Whose fault is this?

BE FRUITFUL, MULTIPLY, FILL THE EARTH
AND CONQUER IT!

Again, I ask, why am I here? The result of an act of violence, no doubt. Just the thought of my mother impaled on my father's rod as it ejaculated me into existence sends me running for the toilet. What devotion to the faith, what Catholicity.

BE FRUITFUL, MULTIPLY … said The Book.

But, wait a second. That's from the OTHER half of The Book, the half we don't talk about (except when it suits us) – the Jewish half.

"Well, then, the priest said so."

"And who is this priest that he should know so much?"

"God told him, he told us, we told you."

Got that? God, GOD, G-O-D said we should.

Fuck that! I want answers, damn it. ANSWERS, not religious propaganda.

OK, all right, I'm whining. I don't like to whine. Let me get it together here. I've got to face the fact; like it or not: I WAS BORN.

But, no, in fact …

I was expelled from my mother's uterus in a rush of mucus and blood on May 25, in the year of Our Tormentor, nineteen hundred and eighty-five. The alien had arrived. After nine months of being referred to as an "it," I was officially given a gender and a name.

Now, I was once naive enough to imagine one's birth certificate was sufficient insurance against the hazards of an identity crisis. To me, a birth certificate was (for all intents and purposes) an official document inscribed in stone. Not so my case, as I came to discover.

Name: Guillermo Fausto Perez III. Nobody calls me this. None of my friends can pronounce it, so instead they call me Rick – don't ask me why. Guillermo also happens to be my father's name, so my family calls me Willie. I guess they figure this way it'll be easier to tell the two of us apart.

Place of birth: Belleview, California. No such city. From what I understand, it was absorbed after my arrival on the planet by the great amoeba Los Angeles. Still, I have to endure inquisitive looks from nail-biting secretaries every time I fill out some kind of application, simply because it's my official birthplace.

Hospital: Belleview Community Hospital. It's not there anymore. Just an open field in East Los Angeles where neighborhood kids run through the weeds chasing a soccer ball.

It's like a bad joke. And it gets worse.

Eight days after I was evicted from The Womb (was I such a bad tenant?), my incurably Catholic parents called in a *mohel* to perform a circumcision on me. Now, just so you don't miss the irony of this, let me explain that a mohel is a Jewish person who specializes in performing ritual circumcision. AND, eight days after the birth of a "manchild" is the time prescribed in Jewish Law for this ceremony, known in Hebrew as *brit milah*.

So why did my Roman Catholic parents do this to me, their first child? Why eight days? Why not six or nine ... or never? And why a mohel?

"It's traditional."

"What tradition? It's a Jewish tradition. I thought we were Catholic."

"It's a family tradition going back a long way, centuries, in fact. What's wrong, you don't like being circumcised?"

"I like it. I LOVE it. I just don't understand ..."

This conversation, and many like it, took place until I was 13. That was the year my grandmother (family historian and guardian of all closeted skeletons) wrecked my life. But more about that later.

My older cousin, Jackie, who wasn't circumcised, used to make fun of my dick all the time. I was forced to change in front of him every time we went swimming at my uncle and aunt's house. "Look at Willie's mushroom head. Hey, Willie boy, what's that fungus you got growing on the end of your ding-dong?"

Then one happy day, quite unexpectedly, Jackie's parents announced he was going to hospital the next weekend – to be circumcised.

My theory is they could no longer endure the fact their son's uncut dick resembled a tapir's snout – they were always such aesthetically minded people. So, at age 15 (I think it was his birthday present), Jackie was force-fed humble pie. Kicking and screaming, Mr High and Mighty was checked into French Hospital in LA's Chinatown, where an uncircumcised Greek doctor surgically peeled his precious dick like a banana.

Three months later, when Jackie's dick was healed enough for him to take it in hand without passing out from the pain, his life returned to normal. I'm sure he hasn't missed a stroke since.

One of my most vivid childhood memories is of being initiated into my parents' peculiar version of Catholicism. I must have been somewhere between two and three years old the day they shrined my room.

The first thing they did was to nail up a palm branch (which had been blessed by a priest during Holy Week) over the doorway of my room. Next came the installation of the three statues that would continue to be my childhood companions until I moved out at 14, when I was sent away to a Catholic boarding school.

The first statue was a life-size (at least it seemed so to me) crucified Christ – very naked and very bloody. My mother told me it was a replica of a Spanish Baroque masterpiece, and that I should feel honored to have it in my room. Looking at it now, as an adult, I have to admit it is a remarkable piece of work. The artist designed it so the compassionate (open) eyes of the dying Christ would be fixed on the penitent – which only worked if the penitent was looking up at it from a certain angle. It took my parents hours to find the "right place" to hang it, and another few days to get the thing to stay up on the wall.

The worst part about it for me was they made me pray to it; they told me I was supposed to love it. No offense, Jesus, but it's not easy to love a naked, bloody man who has just gone through one hell of a Roman torture session when you're only three years old. At that age all the theology doesn't mean much. What stays with you is the image.

Other kids might have dismissed the image, I don't know, but I was scared as hell of it at first. Its eyes followed me no matter where I moved in that room. Sometimes I would hide under the bed to get a little privacy. Most of the time, I slept with my head under the covers. But Bloody Jesus wasn't as bad as the other two statues that made up the trio of relics my parents forced me to sleep with.

There were two nightstands in my room, one on either side of my bed. On one of them stood Saint Lazarus, covered with the oozing sores of leprosy, limping along with the aid of a crutch, followed by four scrubby dogs licking his sores. I was supposed to pray to him, too. On the other nightstand stood the Virgen del Cobre (an apparition of the Virgin Mary in eastern Cuba), rising like Godzilla out of the Caribbean and hovering over three tiny men in a dinghy.

Bloody Jesus, Leprous Lazarus and the Godzilla Madonna – these were my childhood buddies. So what if all the other kids on the block got to share their rooms with Mickey Mouse or the Flintstones, right? I shared my room with the real Masters of the Universe. I could actually talk to my roommates without feeling stupid, and (supposedly) mine could answer.

Eventually I got used to the statues. What I never got used to was the altar at the foot of my bed. This was where my parents lit candles and offered food to "the saints." It works like this: first you take a small table and drape a white sheet over it. Then you load it down with candles and jars of rice and maybe toss in a rosary for good measure. Then you make daily offerings of fruit (usually tropical) or cigars in a jar of water (one of these was put under my bed every other week) or maybe some chicken's blood.

If all this sounds strange to you, like no Catholicism you've ever heard of, it's because my parents were from Cuba, a country whose religious culture is based half on Roman Catholicism and half on African voodoo. The result of this mélange is something called Santeria.

Families involved in Santeria typically belong to a small group of devotees led by a layman priest, in reality a kind of witch doctor. We went to monthly meetings where I witnessed ritual dancing, possessions by saints and all kinds of other public and private goings-on.

I've had a chicken's throat cut over my head; I've had offerings of cigar smoke blown all over my body from the lips of a toothless hag; I've worn amulets around my ankles and around my neck; and I've been masturbated by our Santeria priest in special private counselling sessions – all this in the name of our religious tradition.

If the point of religion is to bestow grace, to free the mind from darkness and to empower the spirit, it didn't work that way for me. Instead, it only served to feed my overactive imagination with images and desires I've only now begun to question and partially understand.

By the time I started puberty – at age 11 – I felt comfortable enough with Jesus, Mary and Lazarus that I felt no shame in regularly whipping out the old dong right there in front of them, under their watchful eyes. No problem. Everything was cool – or so I thought. Then came the night my feel-good session went too far and my dick exploded in my hand. Pus came shooting out of the end and I knew, I just knew, God had finally punished me … I had cancer. Slimy, sticky, white, chlorine-scented cancer of the penis.

I tried wiping up the mess with my pyjama shirt, but it kept oozing out. He wasn't going to let me off so easily. So, tenderly holding my dick in my hand, I carried it into my parents' darkened room and whispered into my (still sleeping) mother's ear, "Momma. Momma, wake up."

She wakes up.

"What's wrong, Willie?"

"Momma, I don't know what happened … but my pee pee … something came out of my pee pee. It looks like pus."

Silence.

"What's wrong?" This is my father waking up now.

"Nothing, you!" says my mother, "Go back to sleep."

She turns back to me and whispers, "Go clean yourself off. You can talk to your father about it in the morning."

"But I tried cleaning it already. It won't stop."

"Clean it again … it'll stop."

"I'm scared, Momma. Am I going to die?"

"You'll be fine. Don't forget to pray first, then go back to bed."

The next day my father took me for a long drive and explained to me all about sex and the changes my body was going through, and he told me: "Try not to rub your pee pee because it's self-abuse," or some such crap. Our little man-to-man had set my mind a bit more at ease. I began to suspect what I suppose I knew all along. God hadn't punished me, and it was probably OK for me to make myself feel good, and maybe even to have my dick explode every once in a while.

Here's where the story gets strange. After months of jerking myself around in bed, I started to have these very weird dreams – sexy dreams that made me come in my sleep. These weren't what you'd call ordinary wet dreams. They were filled with images of violence, death and, of course, sex – kinky sex. And I liked them.

As I got older, my dreams became more (dare I say) sophisticated. The following is a dream I had when I was a sophomore in high school:

There are only two things of which I am aware: the unmistakable strains of a Wagnerian opera and my own heartbeat as I float in total darkness.

Suddenly I find myself walking along the gutter of a downtown street on a foggy night. It's supposed to be London, but it looks like

LA, somewhere near the Greyhound bus terminal on Main Street. The opera continues.

Out of the fog steps a woman with long auburn hair and incredibly tight blue jeans. She beckons me forward with one finger (you guess which one), and I follow her. She looks like my mother, but I ignore that as I follow, enchanted by her beautiful ass, her perfect ass, her divine ass.

I follow (yes, three times I follow in this dream) her ass into an alley. Past the derelicts, past the corners reeking of stale piss, deeper into the alley we penetrate until at last we arrive at a large green garbage bin. The woman reaches out and pulls me behind it.

There, on a discarded old mattress, stained by years of being pissed and come on, we both fall to our knees. I undo the ties of her thin white muslin blouse and out fall her breasts. Breasts as perfect and edible as the ass that goes along with them.

By now the opera is getting real serious (if you know what I mean about German opera). I push her down on her back and start to work my tongue up between her tits. I suck and I bite on her nipples, which by now have grown as hard as jawbreakers.

Out of the corner of my eye I see a rat scuttle past her head. I glance up for a second – just long enough to see a small group of drunks gathering to watch. I don't know if they're attracted by her moans or the music but it's all right ... it makes the incredible sex we perform all the more enjoyable.

Then, as the last movement of the opera reaches its climax, I feel myself undergoing a transfiguration. I'm turning into Richard Wagner – a Richard Wagner with fangs. My lust is transformed into a hunger and I begin to bite her tits harder until they bleed profusely. By this time my young whore is screaming, her screams reflected back by the fog. I gnaw deeper and deeper into her chest, tearing away at what's left of her mammaries with my claws. Having reached her ribcage, I break three ribs off at the sternum, reach into the chest cavity and, pulling out her still beating heart, sink my teeth into it.

The drunks applaud.

Dreams like this fuelled my waking fantasies. It wasn't until I was late in my teens that I realized these were not the fantasies of every red-blooded Hispanic-American boy. This misconception resulted in some embarrassing conversations with girls. The following composite conversation is typical of my 11th-grade summer, the summer I first got to actualize my post pubescent powers. I'll set the scene for you:

Her parents are away for the weekend and I've been invited over for one of my first make-out sessions. We raid the liquor cabinet and try to recreate some forbidden nectar – strawberry daiquiris. Of course, we're both nervous as hell as we settle down next to each other on the living room sofa. I scoot closer to her and feel the warmth of her thigh as it makes contact with my leg. That first physical contact is enough to cause my prick to start inching its way up toward my stomach or down my pant leg. So I decide to get the thing going.

"What's your kinkiest fantasy?"

She smiles. "You really want to hear?"

"Yeah, tell me."

"It's kind of embarrassing."

"Come on, be brave. Tell me," I say, putting my left hand on the inside of her plump right thigh, the way my friends tell me they do it.

"OK ... I've always wanted to have someone ..." here she stops and looks me straight in the eye, then down at my creeping hand.

"You've always wanted someone to what?"

She casts a furtive glance to one side, then back again.

"I've always wanted someone to come in my face and in my hair ..."

A dramatic pause.

"That's embarrassing?" I say.

"... and then lick it off," she says, her face turning the colour of her strawberry daiquiri.

"Hmmm."

"What about you?" she says, "What's your fantasy?"

"I'd like to eat my partner right as she reaches her climax."

She giggles.

"What's so funny?"

"That word, 'partner.' Sounds straight out of a sex manual."

"Sorry."

"No, no, I don't mean it that way. I mean, it's kind of cute." She pulls my hand up higher between her legs, leans over and whispers in my ear, "Besides, you've got the perfect lips for eating a girl out."

"Not eating out. Just eating ..."

"Eating ...?"

"Yeah, you know, EATING – as in 'the black widow eats her young; the praying mantis eats its mate'."

Tense silence. She backs away.

"Forget it," I say. "You'd better finish your drink."

It didn't take too many humiliations of this kind before I learned to keep my fantasies to myself. After all, I didn't see any reason why I should keep freaking out my dates. As long as I didn't actually turn cannibal while we were "doing it," there was nothing to worry about, right? Well ...

Fast-forward to my senior year at UCLA, zipping past six years of sexual debauchery and landing whack in the middle of the era of safe sex and monogamy, I find myself (against my better judgment) about to enter the apartment of one Connie Cash – UCLA's resident nymphomaniac.

Connie is a young librarian type, with great legs and fabulous tits, whom I met in my art appreciation class, notorious for ringing her male classmates to engage in some steamy phone sex. No sooner had we passed around a phone list for everyone in class, than she pounced on the opportunity to begin her telephonic bordello.

The funny thing is nobody, and I mean NOBODY, took her the least bit seriously. Little did she know that before three weeks passed, she had become a sort of joke, a laughing stock among the guys (and some of the women) in the class. Not a week went by that someone didn't have a new Connie Cash story to tell.

I remember the first time she rang me:

"Are you religious?" she says. (This is a classic Connie Cash opening line, which I've already heard from Lance, another guy in our class.)

"Not really," I say, refusing to rise to the bait yet.

"What religion are you?" she says. (Aha! A change in strategy.)

"I'm a narcissist." (I'm playing with her. I think she can sense it.)

"Do you believe in God?" she says, an edge creeping into her voice.

"Sure." (I can't keep this up much longer.)

"So do I." (Here it comes …) "Do you know the first time I knew there had to be a God?"

"I couldn't guess." (Of course, I'm lying.)

"It was the first time I had sex – on the hood of my ex-boyfriend's car."

"Yeah?" (Yawn.)

"Yes, it was a true religious experience …"

And so on.

For some reason I started to enjoy these conversations. Maybe it was the novelty of hearing a 23-year-old coed masturbate herself into a frenzy over Ma Bell's ice cube clear fibre optics; I don't know. But after running up my father's telephone bill, I decided to check out the merchandise in person. That was how I came to be at her door.

I knock once. The door flies opens, and I'm practically knocked on my ass by *Siegfried* pouring into the hallway. Connie sticks her grinning face out the doorway.

"Rick! Don't just stand there. Come inside and give me a hug."

She reaches out and pulls me inside, slamming the door behind me. She folds me in her arms and squeezes me for a full 30 seconds, which gives me an opportunity to quickly check out her apartment. It's nothing like I imagined. No velvet paintings of naked Aztecs (HA!), no erotic art of any kind in fact, only three stuffed unicorns (Huey, Dewey and Louie), a well-stocked bookshelf, a couple of wall posters of the French countryside, and a thundering Wagnerian leitmotif swelling in the background.

"Why don't you turn that shit off," I suggest, prying myself free of her grip.

"Hmmm?"

"The music."

"It's Wagner."

"I know what it is. Turn it off, please."

"You told me you liked classical music!"

"Siegfried is not classical, it's 19th-century German opera. That makes it romantic, not classical."

"But you told me ..." she says, pouting, "I remember you said you liked Wagner."

"Look, Connie, I'm not in the mood for a bunch of screaming Nordics." I move to the stereo and flip it off. "Besides, Wagner puts me in a funny mood."

"Not horny ...?"

"No, just funny. And hungry."

Love at Masada

My father and I drove from Tel Aviv to Masada, in Israel's Judean Desert. We drove mostly in silence, which I didn't mind, because it gave me a chance to look out the window and daydream. The drive through the desert was absolutely exquisite. Having been born and raised in the leafy suburbs of Montreal, I'd never seen such an arid, tortured landscape in all my life.

After what seemed like a long time, we pulled into the car park at Masada, and my father shut off the car. He sat there for a couple of seconds, fidgeting with the hair clip that held his black felt *kipa* in place, not saying anything.

Then he turned to me, looking like a man about to face a firing squad, and opened his mouth:

"I ..."

The moment I heard that first syllable I knew what was coming next, thanks to a well-timed warning from my mother. I wanted to shout at him, "Don't say it, please!" But it was too late. The rest came dribbling out.

"I love you."

It was too pathetic. He'd finally uttered the dreaded words, and there he sat – waiting for my response.

Maybe I should have humoured him by repeating the words back to him. After all, I have to admit that for a guy like him, it must have taken a hell of a lot of courage to try to sell a 13-year-old a crock of shit like that. Anyway, I couldn't say the words; I just couldn't.

I looked at him for a second, trying my best to keep my face empty of any expression, and answered him: "The feeling's mutual ..." It was the best I could do.

His face turned red and I suddenly found myself throttled and slammed repeatedly against the car window.

"Why won't you let me be a father to you!" he yelled.

"Leave me alone, you freak!"

I felt for the door handle with my free hand, and it's a good thing I found it, because he might have killed me if I hadn't. Opening it up, I fell out of the car door to the asphalt and tore through the car park and into a ravine. I hid behind some boulders and cried for a while.

When I saw him a half hour later, he acted as if nothing had happened. We simply got into the car and drove back to Tel Aviv along the same road, in silence. I can remember hating him with every ounce of my being. If I'd been a little older and had a gun, blood would have been shed that day at Masada.

And a Little Child Shall Lead Them

The morning sunlight forced its way through the tattered window blinds and sliced through the dust that hung heavy in the messy bedroom. It focused one particularly intense ray across the face of the woman who lay sleeping on the bed amid a heap of dirty laundry. As the sun pushed upward over the horizon, it stabbed the woman in the eye, waking her from her narcotic slumber. A loud knocking jarred the front door.

"Anyone home? Mrs Hunter?" The knock on the door was insistent. "Mrs Hunter, it's Mrs Jones from next door!"

Sadie Hunter lay on the bed, eyes closed. *I can't move,* she thought. It was much too early for anyone to be calling. Her body was sore, and the morning cold had stiffened her joints. She felt like a bedridden old lady. The knocking continued.

She dragged herself from the warm bed and moved through the clutter of broken furniture to the front door. She unlatched and opened it a crack, peering out at Faye Jones.

"What is it?" she asked the neighbour.

"Are you all right …?" The words echoed dully through her mind. "Mrs Hunter … I asked if you were all right. Floyd and me, we heard the –"

"Mrs Jones, please … yes, of course everything's all right."

"But –"

"Good-bye, Mrs Jones. I told you, everything's fine!"

Sadie slammed the door and listened for a moment. When she was sure the woman had gone away, she moved across the tiny room and looked out of the window. The winter sun continued its way over the eastern ridge, bringing the shantytown into focus. It was early morning but already the coal dust mingled with the mountain mist, creating a brown-tinged ground fog.

Sadie pulled the faded yellow bathrobe closely round her thin frame and gazed out into the distance, transfixed. She would usually start her housework as soon as she awoke, just to keep her mind off the night before. But not this morning. This morning was different.

She walked back to the bedroom and sat opposite the small oak dresser. Her reflection in the mirror startled her. It seemed so foreign to her this morning. Dark bruises marred her complexion and her face was swollen and discoloured. At one time an attractive woman with delicate features, large brown eyes and waist-length black hair, she had become ugly under the pounding blows of her husband's fists. What little dignity she had preserved over the past few months since he had begun his heavy drinking was now evaporating.

Sadie sat before the mirror for several moments, staring at herself. She pulled back the nightgown with one trembling hand to reveal her breasts. There was a dark-purple bruise about two inches above one of her nipples. She palpated the area and bit her bottom lip against the pain. Closing her eyes, she moved her hand down to the nipple and began to knead it gently.

Jack, her husband, had left early to stand in the job line again, the baby was still asleep and Sadie felt quiet ... lost in her thoughts.

It's coming, she thought. Still, she tried to maintain her contemplative mood. *The damned morning freight train.* She could hear it approaching in the distance. It was what bound this town together. One either owned stock in the railroad or worked the mines at the end of the line. And like an artery snaking its way out of the hills and along the outskirts of town, it was the lifeline of this community, a lifeline that never gave and only took ... boxcars full of high-grade coking coal, the guts of these Virginia hills, to be used as fuel in the great smelters up north.

It had taken millions of years of patient pressure to press peat bogs into coalfields but only a few days to rip the coal from the hills and incinerate it in furnaces. All this just to build more trains to haul more coal.

Ignore it, Sadie thought. She wouldn't let it disturb her today.

As the train roared by, it shook every building. Sadie knew what would happen next. She put her fingers in her ears at the moment the engineer let loose a blast on the steam whistle. The baby began to cry. The day had begun.

—ᴍᴡ—

Later in the day, her mother came by. She had always considered it lucky that Sadie had married Jack, given that he came from a good Methodist family. She took one look at Sadie and shook her head disapprovingly.

"What you do to get that husband of yours so riled up I'll never understand." She began looking through the cupboards. "Do you need anything from the store?"

"No, Mother," Sadie said, "I can take care of that myself."

"You certainly can't go out looking like that. Everyone will –"

"Everyone already knows!"

There was a long silence. Both mother and daughter looked steadily at each other across the kitchen table.

Suddenly Sadie buckled over and grabbed her stomach, crying out in pain.

"Honey, what is it? What's wrong?"

"I don't know ... it hurts right here ... like someone's stabbing ..."

"Sit down, dear. Here, let me help you." She lowered her daughter into a small wooden chair. A sweat was breaking out on Sadie's forehead.

"All men have their bad moods, Sadie. Why, your own father, who we all miss, had his bad humours, too. Keep the house clean and have his dinner ready for him when he comes home.

Try to keep him happy, dear. Before you know it, he'll be back to his old self again."

Sadie felt delirious. Her mother's words sounded like a dry hiss. She looked up, no longer recognising the woman standing before her. A sudden panic gripped her chest. She tried to scream but her voice only came out in a whisper.

"Mother –"

"And above all, Sadie" – she picked up an old peach tin that was lying next to the washtub – "try not to provoke him."

"Mother, where are you?"

"I'm right here, dear. Is your stomach hurting again?"

"It's evil, Mother; take it away."

She moved toward Sadie. Sadie recoiled. "Don't touch me."

"Now, Sadie, don't be melodramatic."

"I see snakes, Mother …"

"Snakes …? Where do you see snakes?"

"Everywhere …"

"Now, dear, please get hold of yourself –"

"Jack's new lover is a snake," Sadie said.

"You never told me Jack had found himself a new girl."

Sadie laughed nervously. "He's got a new girl all right … and her name's Gin. They meet each other every night at the tavern. He takes her in his hand and lovingly pours her out into a long, tall glass tumbler, losing himself in her powers. Then she slithers into his mind and, once she's there, she soothes him with her venom, whispering like the little demon that she is, and turns him against me and the baby. Then he stumbles home, with wildfire raging in his eyes."

"Sadie! Stop that!"

"No! Listen … there's more. On those nights, if I so much as look at him, he takes me by the neck –"

"Sadie!"

"By the neck, Mother! He takes me by the neck and flings me across this room. He even tears out my hair –"

"I will not listen to any more of this." Her mother grabbed her handbag and moved toward the front door. "I'm going into town to see the preacher," she called over her shoulder and ran out of the door.

"– in handfuls, Mother. You remember how beautiful my hair was, don't you? Now look at it. And it's all because of snakes." Sadie put her head on the kitchen table and began to sob.

The second train of the morning roared past the shantytown. Its whistle screeched louder and longer than the first. Sadie feared the deafening din was sapping her remaining strength. She looked down at the floor and noticed a few drops of fresh, dark blood. Steam whistle, sharp pain, blood, snakes, train, snakes, blood; Sadie fell from the chair to the whirling, wooden floor and all became darkness.

—⅏—

Toward evening, Pastor Cuthbert knocked on the door. Sadie, now somewhat recovered, had just finished feeding the baby. She automatically opened the door and casually returned to the kitchen. The minister seemed startled by her appearance but managed to compose himself.

"We haven't seen you in town in several weeks, Sadie." He looked down at the little boy, "Hello there, young man."

"Excuse me, Pastor, while I put him to bed," Sadie said unemotionally. She left the minister alone in the kitchen for a few minutes. When she returned, he was leaning against the wall, fidgeting with his hat.

"What is it you wanted?" she asked as she started to clean up the room.

"I just stopped by to see how things were going out here."

"Don't lie, Pastor," snapped Sadie. "I know why you're here."

The minister studied the deathly pale face before him, then spoke again, this time more gravely.

"Your mother tells me you see snakes."

"My mother …" She put down the washrag. "Listen, Pastor, snakes are not the problem."

"Then what is?"

"Look at my face, Pastor," she said. "Does it tell you anything?"

The minister averted his eyes. He drew a long breath, then spoke deliberately.

"We are told that not one sparrow falls to the ground that our Lord is not aware of."

"All right … so he's aware. Now what?"

Again he took a deep pastorly breath, and looked down at his feet.

"Mrs Hunter … it's not my place to interfere in the private affairs of my parishioners, but I can offer some advice." He paused.

"Go on, I'm listening," Sadie said.

Pastor Cuthbert adjusted his pocket watch, looking somewhat annoyed. He seemed at a loss for words.

"He's beat me every night for the past month." Her voice was beginning to tremble.

"Now, Mrs Hunter, that cannot possibly be true. Why, you'd be … dead by now, and we wouldn't let that happen."

The pastor's appearance seemed to Sadie to be changing before her eyes. *He looks like a corpse,* she thought. Sadie's hand tightened on the back of the chair on which she was leaning for support.

"Are you saying I'm lying, Preacher?" she asked weakly.

"Not at all. All I'm saying is that you're obviously shaken up and you may not know exactly what you're saying." He moved forward to take her hands in his. "Come, let's pray together."

Sadie pulled away; the pastor's hands felt cold and lifeless. He looked up at her strangely.

Sadie stared at the talking corpse that stood before her as it leered obscenely. Its jaw moved hungrily as it reached out one of its decaying hands to grab her. *It's evil*, she thought. *I've got to kill it … no, it's already …* She backed up, intent on grabbing the kitchen knife that lay behind, waiting for her, on the table next to the stove.

"Mrs Hunter … are you all right?"

She stopped. The delirium passed as abruptly as it had begun. Pastor Cuthbert edged toward the doorway.

"I don't understand why this thing should happen to you, Mrs Hunter, but I can tell you one thing. A woman's place is one of submission to her husband. If you submit faithfully, as our Lord instructs, I can assure you of his blessings."

"Get out …"

"In the mean time, we will continue to uphold your family in prayer." He moved quickly toward the door.

"How am I supposed to bring up my son in this place, Pastor?" Sadie asked. "We don't even have enough money for a respectable meal."

Pastor Cuthbert stopped, facing the open doorway. "My dear girl," he said, "we all have our crosses to bear." And with that cryptic statement, the minister was swallowed up by the encroaching darkness.

Sadie locked the door.

—ɯ—

Night had fallen and Jack was still not home. This was always a danger signal for Sadie. Jack was sure to be at the tavern tonight.

She looked around the room. Although she'd straightened up the mess earlier, somehow … something still didn't look quite right. Over next to the baby, behind the crib in its usual place, she saw Jack's hunting rifle. It was the most valuable piece of property they owned. They'd bought it back in West Virginia when Jack had decided he was going to take up hunting. It had been at least five years since then, and he still hadn't used it.

"Jack," she'd asked him once, "can't we sell that gun of yours? It's sure to fetch us a good price."

"I told you," he'd answered, glaring, "It ain't a gun – it's a Winchester. And I ain't going to sell it. We ain't that hard-pressed for cash!"

"But you never even use it –"

"That don't make no difference. A hunter never sells his rifle."

He would always do his hunting after he'd been out for a visit, down at the tavern. Afterward, he would come home and pace the room, stalking his imaginary prey like a mountain cat. He would rave for an hour or so then, exhausted, curl up in some corner and fall asleep, holding his beloved Winchester.

She frowned at the rifle. She'd always hated that Jack stored it so close to the baby. Against Jack's specific orders, she picked it up. It felt heavy and cold. It was the first time she'd ever actually held a rifle. Her father had never allowed the girls to touch any of his guns, and Jack had expressly forbidden her to mess with his. A strange sense of dread overcame her at the realisation that this familiar object was both an instrument of provision and of death.

Sadie had never taken the time to think much about death, although, back home in West Virginia, it had always been close at hand, a whispered secret kept safe in dark corners. Death was an alien reality for Sadie. She had never confronted, nor had she been confronted by, her feelings about the subject until now, as she stood there alone, holding the cold steel barrel of her husband's rifle.

Sadie shuddered as she imagined herself a hunted animal, facing its moment of annihilation before a merciless pursuer. She staggered as she felt the bullet penetrate the skin of her breast, shattering the bone of her ribcage, the virgin blood spurting out of the fresh wound, staining the wooden floor a dark crimson, flowing into the corners of the room only to mix with cobwebs and balls of dust. For a moment, she wondered whether she'd accidentally shot herself.

She dragged the rifle to the broom closet and pushed it inside, shutting the door tightly. Then, returning to the bedroom, she checked on the baby.

Kneeling beside his small wooden cradle, Sadie looked at her little boy. His breathing was quiet and regular. She'd forgotten how much she loved to watch him sleeping. It made her feel warm and special, the way she used to feel before the problems began, when they were all happy. She covered him with the warm flannel blanket her mother had made for him.

Sadie studied his tiny face. He had a small indentation in his chin, just like Jack's, and the same slightly turned-up nose. Leaning closer to kiss his forehead, she instinctively caught her breath. It seemed as if he'd stopped breathing, his little face turning a pale blue. She felt a strange mix of fear and relief. Reaching down, she held her trembling hand above his mouth and was startled when he turned over in his sleep. He was fine.

Breathing a long sigh of relief, she closed her eyes for a moment and collected herself. The room was so quiet, so still. Night had shrouded this little corner of Virginia in a darkness rivalled only by the blackness of death, the end of all despair, thought Sadie.

"We all have our crosses to bear ..." She echoed the minister's words, her voice barely audible.

This may well be my cross, she thought, *but I don't think I'm going to carry it much further. I'm not God.*

—⚊⚊—

Jack Hunter spread his cards face up on the poker table. He'd played his last hand.

"Time to go home, Jack?" asked the small balding man with two yellow teeth, who was sitting to Jack's right.

Jack spat on the floor and rubbed the spittle into the ground with his foot. "Guess so," he answered, "if you wanna call that a home."

"Ah c'mon, Jack, yours is one of the better ones out there. At least, it has a wooden floor and real windows," the fat man to his left said.

"I hate it all the same," Jack said, as he poured himself a last swig of gin.

"Why's that?" asked the fat man.

"I should be living in one of them fancy houses on the east side." He laughed hoarsely. "What do those people got that I ain't got?"

"Money," the man with the two yellow teeth said as he broke out into a loud snicker.

"Hell! I had money too, until they threw me out of the mines." There was an uncomfortable pause, as Jack's poker friends heard him rant over the same subject for the third time that evening.

"'Two months!' they told me. 'Don't worry, Jack, business is slow now. You'll be back in the mines in no time.' Well, 'no time' must mean 'never', because six months has passed and I still ain't heard a word."

"Seems to me you sort'a drank yourself out of that job," the fat man said.

"They know I got a family to feed." He became angry at the thought of his family. "Shit, tossed out of his job and that woman of mine has to go and have herself a baby."

"All right, gentlemen," called out the bartender, "10 minutes to closing time."

The men around the poker table exchanged glances as Jack stared into his empty glass. The young man across from him decided to break the silence with a little joke.

"Hey, Jack, you lose something in there?"

Red eyed and cocked like a loaded gun, Jack looked up at the young man, "You trying to make me look stupid, boy?"

"No. Just trying to lighten things up a bit, that's all," answered the young man, with an almost polished nonchalance.

Jack leaned forward in his chair, like a viper ready to strike. "You watch your mouth, boy, or you'll be swallowing your teeth, silver and all."

Unblinking, the young man answered, "I reckon you get a whole lot of practice at home, messing up your wife."

"Why you little –" Jack sprung at the young man but was yanked back into his chair by the men who'd come to the table to listen to the argument. He struggled for a moment, but soon lost his will to fight as the gin raced to his head.

"What kind of life is it when a man's business ain't even private no more?" he moaned.

"He didn't mean nothing by it, Jack," the fat man said. "It's that old Faye Jones, Floyd's woman. Why, she's been cackling all over town about how you tear up the house every night."

"That's right, Jack," the yellow-toothed man said. "She's the one who said it first."

"That bitch … she don't know nothing about what's going on. None of you do! You don't know what it's like comin' home night after night to a wife and kid, without nothing to give them … barely enough even to eat."

The bartender moved to Jack's side and took him by the arm. "C'mon, Jack, why don't you go on home."

Jack shook himself free. "No, wait a second, damn it! I want you guys to know … Sadie, she … she's been getting all quiet and sad lately. I hate looking at that face of hers, listening to her talk. I mean, she gets into these real morbid moods –"

As he spoke of Sadie, Jack felt a strange sensation, a cold premonition that something awful was happening back home. He rose to his feet. "I've gotta go," he said.

The men exchanged puzzled glances.

"Jack, what is it … what's wrong?" asked the bartender.

"Something … I don't know," Jack said, as he ran out of the door and into the road.

"At least close the door, Jack; you're lettin' all the warm air out."

"Hey, Jack, go home and sleep it off ..."

He no longer recognised the voices. He felt only the need to hurry home, drawn by the premonition that something terrible was happening.

He staggered down the road toward the shantytown that lay west of the rails, where he lived. A light drizzle had begun to fall, dampening his face. This was the kind of rain that did little to refresh. Things looked dirtier after this kind of rain. Jack hated it, as he hated most everything when he was drunk.

The gas lamp at his back cast long, shifting shadows on the uneven, gravel road. A rising wind raked clouds across the sky and the light of the full moon broke through every now and then, animating the landscape. Jack moved through the centre of town, now devoid of people, down the middle of State Street.

He passed the Opry House just as the bell in the church tower was chiming 10 o'clock. Well-dressed townspeople were pouring out into the street. Red eyed, he looked upon them with contempt. He thought he saw the preacher in the crowd. "Shit," he said, and kicked a clod of dirt. They made plenty of room for Jack Hunter to stumble past.

As he neared the edge of town, he passed the local cathouse and instinctively felt his pockets; they were empty. All the lights were on upstairs. Business had been slow here, too.

He felt a sick, churning feeling in his stomach begin to work its way upward. Just as the rain began to come down in sheets, Jack stepped around to the side of an old Victorian house and vomited. He found himself soaked and now ravenous. Wiping his mouth on his sleeve, he picked up his pace as he continued down the road.

Up ahead, around a bend in the road, lay the tracks, where a freight train was lumbering past. He stood at the tracks and waited for, what seemed to him, hours. The last car finally passed, revealing the shantytown below, at the bottom of a shallow ravine. He saw it as if for the first time – a collection of about

150 ramshackle homes, made out of anything their owners could lay their hands on. His feeling of apprehension increased as he staggered down the hill and approached his house.

Sadie would always leave a lighted lantern for him on the front porch when night fell, but tonight both the porch and the front room were dark. Cautiously, he approached the steps but lost his balance. He tripped on a loose board and fell hard on his knees, ripping his well-worn trousers. His anger flared. "Damn!" he swore, as he rose to his feet. He moved to the door and tried to open it. It was locked. He rapped loudly on the doorpost but there was no answer.

"Open up, Sadie, it's me!"

The door didn't open. He rapped harder, until it seemed to him he'd rapped his knuckles raw.

"Goddammit, woman, open up!"

He lurched out and kicked the door. He could hear the baby crying inside.

In the darkness he thought he could make out the neighbours peering at him from behind their cardboard curtains. He could imagine their words. "Yes, sir, just look at how Sadie Hunter's locked out her Jack in the rain ..." The bile was rising in his throat. *Hang it all*, he thought, *I'll bust it down.*

Throwing himself at the door, he noticed with satisfaction that the wood in the frame was starting to crack. It was an old, weathered door and would come down in no time. He hurled his body at the door a second time. The house shuddered. One more time and he'd be inside. He backed up five paces and ran at the door, full force. The house shook to its foundations as the door fell in, and Jack on top of it.

He lay sprawled on the floor for a second or two, face down and knocked half out of his senses. He lifted his head. Through the clearing dust he saw that the front room was empty. He could still hear the baby crying, although now the crying seemed to be coming from further back in the house, in the bedroom.

Something was definitely wrong. He crept forward. The door to the bedroom was ajar; the light of a kerosene lamp flickered inside. Stepping into the bedroom, Jake saw that, except for the baby, the room was empty. He dashed to the cradle, intending to grab his rifle from behind it, when he heard the bedroom door click shut. Wheeling around, he found himself staring straight into the barrel of his Winchester, which Sadie held, aimed carefully at his head; her face, expressionless. She spoke slowly, deliberately.

"You missed your dinner."

Outside, the shriek of a whistle split the night, as a passing freight train rocked the shantytown, carrying another load of coal into the darkness.

Star Party

27 July 1995; 22.00
Mount Tamalpais, Marin County, California
Rock Springs, just east of Highway 30

"**M**y God, just look at that!" My boyfriend Isaac made a couple of quick adjustments on his jet-black refractor telescope and backed away from the eyepiece, a wide grin on his face. "You'll find it right in the centre of the viewfinder."

A young woman crunched past us on the gravel, dragging her fat white reflector telescope behind her. I could barely make out her rounded cherub face in the dark. "Hey, Isaac," she whispered, "glad you made it."

"Oh hey, Claire," Isaac whispered back, "this is my friend, Marc."

Claire peered in my direction and waved. "Welcome to star central, Marc," she said. "Isaac, do you think you could … this thing is kind of heavy."

"Sure, not a problem." Isaac squeezed my arm and walked over to help Claire set up her telescope in one of the less congested spots of the scrub field.

I squinted in the dark and scanned the large gathering of people that made up that evening's star party. There were more than 50 individuals present, amateur astronomers who gathered together once a month, far from the lights of the city, to gaze heavenward. The rest of us were the curious invitees and spouses, who tagged along.

Star parties. Despite the name, these were quiet events, the only sounds audible being the buzz of crickets, the soft crunching of gravel underfoot and the low murmur of conversation. The usual star party procedure was thus: each amateur astronomer would train his telescope on whichever part of the sky interested him. Each would then receive visitors at his telescope. It was not unlike holding court. Other astronomers or their guests would each take a turn to look into this or that person's telescope, and would be expected to listen while the telescope owner expounded on this star cluster, that planet or that galaxy.

This was the usual procedure. But tonight was different. Tonight the telescopes of all amateur astronomers the world over were trained on one object, and one object alone.

I took off my glasses, leaned forward against the eyepiece and felt the cool circle of metal around my eye as my vision attempted to adjust to the magnification. I was having trouble seeing anything other than the reflection of my own eyelashes.

Isaac crunched back across the gravel and stood behind me. "So, what do you think?"

"I can't see anything. It all looks black." I moved away from the telescope.

Isaac frowned and looked into the eyepiece, made a few adjustments, then turned the telescope over to me again. "That should be better. Only this time hold your head still, look straight into the centre and try not to nudge the scope."

I looked again, making sure to not angle my eye off to the side. This time I saw them: the stars, a few planets, impossibly distant galaxies. They showed up as sharp or fuzzy points of light against the silky black background of space.

"All right, I'm seeing stars. Now what?"

"Focus your eye on the big fuzzy ball in the center. Do you see it?"

"Yeah, I see that. What is it?"

"That's M70 … a globular cluster. Now, look a bit to the left of M70."

"OK, I'm looking."

"What do you see?"

There it was. I was surprised to find my heart was racing, my breath shortening. I hadn't expected to have a physical reaction to a small, fuzzy image of light in a telescope, something so easily missed by the uninitiated. But there it was, ever so distant and yet unmistakable: the comet.

Having been simultaneously sighted only five nights ago by two amateur astronomers (one in New Mexico, the other in Arizona), the powers-that-be in the world of astronomy had already named it – after both of them: Hale-Bopp. The Hale-Bopp comet was now the latest astronomical sensation.

"It's incredible," I said. "I can just make out the tail and ..." I backed away from the telescope. "How far away did you say it is?"

"More than 650 million miles. And it's headed straight for us." Isaac raised one eyebrow slyly behind the horn-rimmed glasses that gave him his intriguing professorial look. "It's not likely to strike the earth. They say it will probably make a close pass in a couple of years. We'll see."

I looked back into the eyepiece. This time I had no trouble locating the comet, a tiny pinpoint of light with an even tinier smudge of light trailing behind it. As I took in the amazing sight, I felt Isaac moving up behind me, his warm breath close on my neck and, a moment later, a light kiss. I backed away slowly from the eyepiece.

"Your friends will see," I said.

Isaac laughed. "Who cares?" He kissed me more passionately, this time on the mouth. "Do you think it matters what anyone thinks?"

"Well, it depends on whom, I suppose."

"Nope," he said playfully, "one day we'll all be gone. The sun will nova and all this will disappear in one searing flash. And what we did or didn't do won't matter to anyone, because no one will be left."

"Thank you, Mr Astronomer," I said, and affectionately returned the kiss.

We were interrupted by a light crunch-crunch followed by the clearing of someone's throat. We looked up to see Bob Jamsheet, the star party's 40-something coordinator. "Hello, my friends." Jamsheet's ultrawhite teeth shone in the dark as he smiled blissfully at us. It struck me that every time I'd ever seen him, he was smiling. It seemed to me he was perpetually on the verge of nirvana.

"Oh hi, Bob," Isaac said. He wiped his mouth with the back of his hand. "Have you met my friend, Marc Sadot?"

Jamsheet bowed ceremoniously in my direction. "Yes, certainly I've had the pleasure of meeting your friend. You are well, Mr Sadot?"

I bowed back. "Thank you, yes, I'm doing fine, Bob."

"Wonderful," he said, his smile morphing into a full-blown grin. "I was wondering, Isaac, if you would be interested in discussing some of the future events we have planned for the group."

"Yes, sure …"

Jamsheet bowed again. He withdrew a small spiral notebook from the breast pocket of his Nehru jacket and leafed through a few pages.

"You mean now?"

"If it's not too much trouble, Isaac. I believe now is as opportune a time as any."

"I'll take a walk," I said to Isaac. "I'm curious to see how the comet looks in some of the other telescopes."

Jamsheet smiled and nodded at me as I left him and Isaac to review the group's agenda.

I picked my way across the field to where Claire's telescope was set up and found her squatting next to it in a nest of chaparral. She was looking up into the starry sky and nursing a cup of something hot and steaming.

"Did you get tired of looking through the telescope?" I said.

Claire turned her head and blinked at me. "It's prettier this way." She extended an open hand skyward and indicated the broad band of stars that made up the edge of the Milky Way. "It's like a carpet of diamonds."

I looked up and nodded. "Yeah, it is kind of like that, isn't it?" I pointed at her oversized reflector. "May I?"

"Be my guest … It's not actually focused on anything."

I laughed and looked into the eyepiece. Then I realised she wasn't joking. I looked at her questioningly.

She sneered at the telescope. "Why get all hung up over a couple of trees when you can lose yourself in the whole forest?"

"OK … I guess I see your point …" I squatted next to her. "So why the telescope, why even come to the star party?"

Claire shrugged. "Don't mind me. I'm just pissed off about something. Want some Ovaltine?"

"Ovaltine? I haven't had that since I was a kid. It isn't spiked with something, is it?"

Claire sniggered and pulled out a little metal flask from under her backpack. "Only a bit of spiced rum. How'd you know?" She opened it and passed it under my nose. A strong scent of vanilla pierced my brain and I pulled back. Claire laughed again. "Want some?"

"Sure, OK, I'll have some Ovaltine but I'll pass on the rum, if it's all the same to you."

She frowned and pushed out her bottom lip in an exaggerated pout. "Fine, Mr Straight-Laced Lawyer. One hot virgin Ovaltine coming up." She fished a coffee mug out of her backpack, filled it with steaming liquid from out of a lunchbox-style Thermos, and pushed the mug at me.

I sniffed at the contents. "Are you sure this is Ovaltine?"

Claire turned away from me and looked back up at the sky. "I'm afraid you'll have to trust me on that."

I took a tentative sip of the hot drink. It was, indeed, Ovaltine or, if not, something chocolaty nonetheless. Good enough. I sat next to her. "Thanks."

She flashed me a thumbs-up.

"So ..." I said after a moment, "what's bothering you, if you don't mind my asking?"

"So ..." she echoed back, "what kind of law do you practise?"

"Who said I was a lawyer?"

"Isaac told me, of course," she said, a tone of exasperation creeping into her voice. "What he didn't tell me was what kind of law you practise."

"I see."

"So ... What kind of law –"

"I'm a litigator. I prosecute civil cases against companies that discriminate against their employees, or that allow their supervisors to sexually harass their employees."

"Sounds complicated," Claire said. She took a swig of rum from the flask and looked away.

"You weren't really interested in that, were you?" I said.

"Not really, no."

I stared at Claire for a while, wondering why I even cared about the obviously miserable mood she was in. I didn't even know the woman. And yet, I didn't feel comfortable about simply walking away from her.

"Sure you don't want to talk or something?" I said.

Claire lowered herself to the ground and stretched her legs out in front of her. She knocked her shoes together a couple of times and a little cloud of dust rose from them into the air. "I'm pissed off because my boyfriend called me a nerd this afternoon."

"Oh ..."

"He didn't want me to come up here tonight. He thinks all my friends are freaks and now he thinks I'm one, too." She looked at the telescope with something like hate in her eyes and then, ever-so-slowly, edged her feet close to it until they were touching one of the telescope's tripod legs. "You don't think I'm a freak, do you, Mr Lawyer?"

"What I think is that you've had a little too much of that rum."

Claire smirked at me and took another swig from the flask. She tapped a foot against the telescope's tripod leg.

"You don't want to do that," I said.

She stared at me for a moment, looking for all the world like she was about to give her poor telescope a good hard shove. I readied myself to come to the rescue of the poor unoffending reflector. And then, as if reacting to a sudden change of heart, Claire sullenly pulled back her foot, replaced the cap on the flask, packed it away in her backpack and drew up her knees. "Like I said, don't mind me. I'm pissed off."

I released a long breath and regarded her out of the corner of my eye. "Why didn't you bring him with you?"

"Who, my boyfriend?" Claire knocked on the top of her head with her fist a couple of times. "He is so not into this," she said. "This is my trip. We're not exactly the perfect, most compatible couple, you know. Not like Isaac and you, you lucky bastards."

She looked up above my head and waved cheerily at someone behind me. "Hello, Isaac, we were just talking about you."

I turned around and found Isaac standing directly behind me, looking unusually glum. I scooted to one side to make room between Claire and me. "Isaac, I didn't hear you come up. Pull up a seat," I said.

Isaac squeezed in between us and leaned his head heavily on my shoulder.

"Oh, my God," Claire said. "Aren't you two the picture of marital bliss? Quick, let me grab my camera and snap a picture of the happy couple."

Isaac held up a hand and waved her off. "Please, Claire, back off, I'm not in the mood –"

"No wait, how many years did you tell me the two of you have been together now? Four years, right? Or was it 10?"

Isaac sat up and glared at her. "It's four years, thank you. Now, would you please back off, Claire. I'm not kidding."

Claire opened her mouth to say something, but then thought the better of it and shrugged.

"What's the matter?" I asked Isaac.

"Later," he muttered.

Claire cocked her head to one side and looked at Isaac. He averted his eyes. She reached out and brushed aside a lock of hair that had fallen across his face. "Sorry to be such a pain," she said.

Isaac looked at her for a moment, then shook his head. "It's not you. It's the group. Bob's just told me about a trip he's planning for later this year."

"Yeah, so?" Claire said. "What about it?"

"To see the aurora borealis."

"Oh, yeah? How fantastic!" she said. "I've always wanted to see it."

"That is precisely the problem ... I've always dreamed about seeing it, too. But I can't."

"Why not?"

Isaac looked at me and raised an eyebrow. "You tell her," he said.

I searched his face to see if he genuinely wanted me to discuss his situation with Claire.

"Tell me what?"

"Go ahead, it's all right," he said to me.

"Isaac's here in the United States on a temporary grant of asylum. Until his final case is decided, he's not allowed to leave the country."

Claire crinkled her brow and looked down for a moment.

Isaac nodded. "It's like I'm being held prisoner here. We can't travel like normal people. You know, sometime I'd like to take a trip abroad, even to Tijuana ... just over the border. Or to Vancouver."

"How long have you been waiting for an answer?" she asked.

"I applied back in 1985, the year I arrived. Ten years ago! And I'm still waiting."

I put my hand on his back and rubbed between his shoulder blades, in the spot where his tension usually accumulated. "There are other places we can go while you're waiting, here in the United States. You don't have to go see the aurora –"

"I want to go, Marc. I've always dreamed about seeing the aurora borealis, and now Bob and everyone else, they're all going to go – and I can't."

"We'll go, don't worry about it, one of these days –"

"What would happen if you left the United States?" Claire asked.

"He'd be barred from coming back in and his application for asylum would be automatically denied. Basically, he'd be up shit creek with nowhere to go except back to El Salvador."

Claire took Isaac's hands into her own and squeezed them. He looked at her, looking close to tears. "Isaac, listen to me. You don't have much of a choice except to wait, do you?"

Isaac looked down and shook his head. "I'm tired of the whole thing, not being able to plan for the future ..." he looked up at me, "our future."

"If it will make you feel any better," said Claire, "I'll put off going to see the aurora until we can go see it together."

Isaac laughed half-heartedly. "You don't have to do that, Claire. Besides, you may be waiting a long time."

"Not a problem for me," she said, "I've survived 25 years without seeing it, a few more years won't make that big a difference in the cosmic scheme of things."

Isaac smiled. "True enough." He kissed her on the cheek. "You're a good friend."

Claire smiled back at him, then rubbed her face vigorously with both hands. "I'm cold, boys. I think I'm going to call it a night. How about you?"

I stood and brushed the dust off my jeans. "I'm ready. How about you," I said to Isaac, putting my hand on the crown of his head.

He looked around the scrub field. "Yeah, it looks like people are starting to pack it up." He pulled me close and gave me a hug. When he finally released me, he said: "I'm going to help Claire pack up her telescope. Why don't you pull the car up to that big cypress tree. I'll be there in a few minutes."

Claire ran up to me as I moved away. "Hey, Marc, wait up a second ..."

I looked at her.

"I want to apologise for breaking your balls earlier," she said. "I know I was being a real pain."

"Sure, thanks, Claire ... We all have our bad days."

She hopped from one foot to the other, looking like she wanted to say something else.

"By the way, thanks for that, back there," I said. "That was very nice of you."

She shook her head. "He's a friend. And he's put up with a lot of my crap."

I smiled at her and started toward the car.

"Marc ..." she said.

I turned around. She approached me, looking back quickly before speaking. "How much longer do you think, until he gets an answer on his case?"

"I have no idea. Maybe this year, maybe never."

"Oh ..."

"It was a pleasure meeting you – finally."

When I got to the car I looked back and saw Claire still standing in the same place I'd left her, gazing up at the sky, lost in her carpet of diamonds.

An Israel State of Mind, Part I

Eighteen-year-old Marc Sadot opened his eyes as the captain of El Al flight 208 announced the beginning of its 20-minute descent to Tel Aviv. He squinted out of the window into the darkness and imagined that the plane was now flying over the Mediterranean, somewhere off the coast of Lebanon or Northern Israel. In the distance, at the far edge of the horizon, he could make out a lightening of the sky, a faint pink tinge signalling the approach of dawn.

He felt a rustling next to him and glanced in the direction of his girlfriend and travel companion, Lisa Katz. She was languidly suppressing a yawn with one hand and rubbing the sleep out of her still closed eyes with the other. The large barrette that held her wavy auburn hair in a thick ponytail had snapped open sometime during the flight, and her hair now covered half her face. Marc turned away from her and looked out the window expectantly. The dawn was advancing, and the sky was growing lighter by the minute.

A moment later, the captain switched on the cabin lights and Marc found himself staring at his own reflection in the Plexiglas. He had recently cut his long hair into a low-maintenance crew cut in preparation for the trip, and was pleased with the way the new style set off his deep-set black eyes and aquiline features.

"What are you looking at?" Lisa asked, taking hold of his hand and imposing her head on his shoulder. "Can you see anything yet?"

Marc averted his eyes from his reflection and focused on the horizon. The silvery waters of the Mediterranean and a distant, indistinct coastline were coming into sharp focus.

"We'll be there soon," he said, disengaging his fingers from Lisa's moist hand and rubbing them against his jeans.

She smiled mischievously at him. Then, with a quick glance around to make sure nobody was looking, she let the palm of her hand drop into his lap. He frowned and placed his hand on top of hers.

"Not now, Lise …"

"No one's looking," she said.

Marc grabbed her wrist firmly. "That'd be three times. It's enough."

Lisa extricated her hand from his painful grip. "You've never complained before," she said, a bit too loud.

"Will you please keep your voice down," he said, looking around at the other passengers. "You don't need to make a scene."

"Fine. I won't make a scene if you let me –"

Marc unfastened his seatbelt and climbed out of his seat, moving in the direction of the aisle.

"Where are you going?" Lisa asked, pulling on his shirt.

"Let go of me." He yanked his shirt out of Lisa's grasp. "I'm going to the toilet."

Marc dashed down the aisle and popped into the first unoccupied lavatory he could find. After latching the door behind him, he lowered the toilet seat and sat on it with a mournful shake of his head. His heart was racing, and a hot sweat was breaking out on his forehead. *Breathe deep,* he thought to himself. *Don't let this turn into another panic attack.* Placing one hand on his chest and the other on his stomach, he began to breathe, using the yoga techniques he had read about in a book he recently found in the library.

Just 22 hours before, as he was finishing packing, he'd felt sure he would be able to handle this trip to Israel with Lisa. It wasn't quite what he had planned. Far from it. This was supposed to have been a solo trip for him, a rite of passage after high school. But then, inevitably, his mother had gotten involved, and then Lisa's mother and, before he knew it, the arrangements had been made. And here he was now.

But the real wild card, the thing that was causing Marc the greatest anxiety, was the fact that he and Lisa were being sent to Kibbutz Kfar Vered in the upper Galilee to join Lisa's older brother, Simon. The mere thought of Simon caused Marc's pulse rate to increase. Simon and he had a history, a dirty little secret history that had begun when Marc was only 12 years old and Simon a blossoming adolescent of 15. That history had lasted until the year Simon left for Israel, exactly one year ago. After a year of dealing with the sexual confusion and the separation, Marc was dreading the prospect of facing Simon once again.

A loud knock at the lavatory door brought him back to the present. He rose from the toilet seat, splashed a bit of lukewarm water on his face, then returned to his seat, barely acknowledging Lisa as he slid past her and sat next to the window.

"What's wrong?" she asked.

"Nothing's wrong. Just leave me alone for a bit."

She studied him for a few seconds and, as she did, her eyes came to rest, as if for the first time, on the dark-blue knitted *kipa* on his head. She reached over and pulled threateningly on it.

"You should take that thing off. Your father's not watching you now."

Marc slapped her hand away. "I'm not wearing it for him."

"Ouch, you brute." Lisa rubbed her hand. "It's not cool to be religious at the kibbutz we're going to. People are going to assume you're religious if you go around wearing that."

Marc resecured the kipa with a tiny hair clip and turned away from Lisa to look out of the window.

"You know," she said after a moment, "if you keep on ignoring me like that, I'm liable to find myself a new boyfriend at the kibbutz."

"Go ahead," Marc muttered, "it wouldn't surprise me if you did."

Fifteen minutes later, the plane made hard contact with the runway at Ben Gurion International Airport and rolled several hundred metres before the pilot engaged the air brakes and brought the 747 to a wrenching halt.

A collective sigh of relief erupted from all 233 passengers, some of them spontaneously breaking into applause. A young man wearing a Queen T-shirt and a denim kipa leapt out of his seat and lead his section of the cabin in a raucous version of *Havenu Shalom Aleichem*. As the plane taxied to the disembarkation area, most of the rest of the passengers took up the tune, accompanied by rhythmic hand-clapping.

Marc opted out of the celebration and instead took in his first view of Israel through the small window with a sense of fascination. He couldn't see much beyond the white stucco terminal buildings, which reflected back the bright morning sun. Nevertheless, he felt as if he were entering an utterly different world from the one he had left in Southern California.

Lisa nudged him with her elbow. "Come on, you stick-in-the-mud. Sing!"

He turned his head in her general direction and watched with mild amusement as she sang and clapped with the rest of the passengers. After a moment, he let out a sigh and turned away once again to look out of the window.

The plane was taxiing toward a set of airstairs. At the bottom of the stairs, standing at full attention, Marc could see a soldier wearing a green IDF uniform and a black beret, holding an Uzi submachine gun at a 45-degree angle across his chest. Marc crinkled his brow and pressed his face against the Plexiglas to get a better look.

The singing subsided and, despite clear instructions from the flight crew, many of the passengers leapt out of their seats and caused a general chaos in the aisles by extracting their carry-on luggage from the overhead bins. Marc continued to stare out of the window.

"Now what are you looking at?" Lisa said, struggling to pull a hairbrush through her tangled auburn mane.

"There's a soldier out there," Marc said, his eyes glued on the soldier. "He's got a machine gun."

Lisa tried unsuccessfully to edge her head into the small window space. "Where? I can't see anything except your big head."

Marc turned and cut his eyes at her. Lisa chuckled maliciously and pressed her face toward the window. "I do so love to push your buttons."

"I've noticed."

"Ooh, he's cute." Lisa turned and smiled at Marc. "Dangerous looking, too."

The plane finished pulling up alongside the airstairs and came to a complete stop. A flight attendant threw open the door to the craft, which opened with an audible hiss, and, with the assistance of the ground crew, secured the airstairs to the fuselage. The passengers pushed down the aisles toward the exit.

Marc yanked up his armrest and slid past Lisa. She shifted into his seat and continued looking out of the window. "I'm serious," she said, "that guy's proper cute."

Marc waited for a break in the flow of passengers and moved into the aisle, snatching up his backpack and allowing himself to be pushed toward the exit. "Let's go," he called over his shoulder to Lisa. "We're deplaning."

Lisa pulled her face out of the window and saw that Marc was half-way to the exit.

"Wait up!" she called.

But Marc kept walking. When he stepped out of the plane he was assaulted by the summer heat and the intense glare of the morning. He extracted a pair of Wayfarers from his backpack, installed them over his eyes and moved down the stairs.

As he reached the tarmac, he stole a long look at the soldier. He was perhaps a year or two older than Marc and stood a good four inches taller. His blue-black hair was cropped short and his handsome face was tanned a deep brown. But the soldier's intense green eyes were the feature that most caught Marc's attention. They seemed fixed on some very distant object beyond the horizon.

Marc lifted his sunglasses and nodded a greeting at the soldier but the soldier ignored him and continued to stare straight ahead. An elderly man behind Marc impatiently pushed past him and scurried toward the single-file line that was forming to enter the terminal building. Marc shrugged and moved on.

Just as he reached the door of the terminal building, Lisa caught up and pushed her way into the line behind him. Angry passengers shook their heads and uttered mild curses at her in English, Hebrew, Yiddish, French, Russian.

"Hey, what's the big idea?" she said to him, gabbing hold of his shirt.

Marc closed his eyes then, drawing a deep breath, pressed into the building and found himself inside a large hangar-like room jammed with hundreds of people trying to make it past a mere four Israeli immigration officers.

"My God," Lisa said, as she was pulled in behind him. "This is going to take hours."

"Watch your language," Marc muttered.

"Excuse me, Mr Rabbi's son." She dropped her backpack to the floor with a heavy thud and dragged it behind her. "I swear, sometimes I think you're a closet puritan."

"I'm not a closet anything," he snapped, and then quickly manoeuvred to a part of the crowd that seemed to be making at least some minimal progress toward one of the checkpoints. Lisa followed at his heels.

"Anyway," she said, "that soldier back there ... he smiled at me."

"He did not."

"All right, he didn't. But he wanted to. I could tell."

Marc inched forward, still at least 20 minutes away from the immigration checkpoint, and tried to concentrate on the next few days that lay ahead. But all that kept coming to his mind was the image of the soldier at the foot of the stairs – the distant, almost wild look in his eyes. Marc felt a sudden tinge of envy and then, just as suddenly, he felt ashamed.

Lisa bounced up and down on her toes. "This isn't a funeral, you know. You should be more excited. We're really here!"

Marc turned and looked at her, his face expressionless.

"I'm tired," he said. "Try to keep a lid on your enthusiasm until after I've had a chance to take a nap and a shower."

Lisa stopped bouncing and pushed out her lower lip. "Sorry, boss."

After they cleared immigration, they spent a few minutes freshening up in their respective washrooms and met each other, as planned, in front of the terminal building. A slow-moving river of honking automobiles and taxis rolled past, and the smell of diesel was overpowering. Marc motioned Lisa back inside.

"Where did your brother say we'd find those … what do you call them?" he asked, when they had reached a place of relative quiet.

She extracted a crumpled piece of paper from one of the various pockets of her khakis and flattened it out against the wall.

"Umm, *sheruts*," she said. "They're called *sheruts*."

"Where do we find them?"

"It says here that if we go out of the terminal doors and veer to our right, we'll find a special parking lot for them. And that we should ask for one that goes to Kfar Vered."

They jogged to their right along the pavement that skirted the terminal until they ran out of concrete and found themselves standing in a gravelly, traffic-choked parking lot. People were loudly negotiating fares and destinations with various hard-looking drivers. Marc approached a low wooden booth and found a desiccated old man inside, sitting backward in a rickety chair and picking his teeth with a thick splinter of wood.

"Excuse me," Marc said. "We're trying to get to Kfar Vered."

"Grandpa doesn't speak English," came a husky voice from behind.

Marc whirled around and found a wiry-haired, heavy man towering over him.

"Oh, sorry," Marc said. "My girlfriend and I, we're trying –"

"I heard you. You want to go to Kfar Vered." He pulled a rumpled cigarette from behind his hairy ear and pointed it at a big brown car, parked at the extreme edge of the parking lot surrounded by a small crowd. "Giddy will take you, and those people, too."

Marc and Lisa approached the car and found six young people, backpacker types like themselves, bargaining a fare with a bored, mop-haired driver, who was sitting sideways in the driver's seat, his long legs and sandalled feet thrust out of the door. He didn't look like he was in a hurry to go anywhere.

"No, that is not correct," the driver was saying to one of the backpackers, an exasperated-looking freckly young man. "It's 530 shekels to go as far as Kfar Vered. Not more and not less."

"But, I already told you, we're not going that far," argued the young backpacker, pulling on his red hair in frustration.

"Yes, you've already told me. 'Only as far as Tiberius.' But if you ride in this sherut, all of you together, as a group, you will pay me 530 shekels. Divide it up among yourselves however you like."

Lisa elbowed her way through the small crowd until she was nearly standing between the driver's long legs. "Excuse me there, but do you have room for two more?"

The driver shielded his eyes from the sun with one hand and squinted up at Lisa. After a moment, his face broke into a broad smile and he got out of the car. The man stood at least six feet three inches tall and was built like a spider monkey. He reached out a long thin arm toward Lisa.

"Well, hello there," he said. "Welcome to Israel. I'm Gideon. And you are …?"

Lisa took his hand and returned his smile. "We're going to Kfar Vered … my boyfriend and I. Do you have room for us?"

"But of course, I have room for a lovely young lady like you." He turned to the freckle-faced young man and his companion with a twisted smile. "Looks like you'll have to find some other way of getting to Tiberius, my friends."

The young man and his friend fired off a few choice swear-words at the driver in Arabic and stormed off toward the booth, giving the sherut a swift kick on the rear bumper as they passed it.

"Now," the driver said, turning back to Lisa and devouring her with his large brown eyes, "the fare is normally 530 shekels per load."

"Perfect," Marc said, taking Lisa by the arm. "Five hundred and thirty shekels it is."

"One moment, please. Young lady," the driver said, holding up the palms of both hands as if surrendering. Lisa turned back to him. "As I was saying, the fare is normally 530 shekels. But, I'm willing to take 320 – that's only 54 for each of you – if you will do me the honour of riding in the front seat, next to me."

"Forget it, brother," Marc said. "Come on, Lise."

"Hey, that's almost half price!" one of the other backpackers called out. "Let her sit up front, man."

"Come on, Marc," Lisa said, never taking her eyes off the driver.

"Yes, come on, Marc," the driver said with a gleam in his eye. "It's only a ride. You can even sit up front next to her."

Marc pulled on Lisa's arm, but she held firm. He looked around for a moment at the others.

"Don't worry, religious boy," the driver said, indicating the other passengers with a flourish. "Nothing will happen to your girlfriend – not with all these excellent chaperones and yourself to supervise."

"See, what did I tell you?" Lisa whispered out of the side of her mouth. "He thinks you're religious. Take that thing off."

In the end, Marc was forced to capitulate by majority vote, his being the only nay vote. The experience left him so angry with Lisa for, as he put it, "selling yourself to a tacky taxi driver for 54 lousy shekels," that he didn't want to even look at her, much less sit next to her. So he gave up his front seat to one of the backpackers and squeezed into the back with the other two.

"Not a good choice, that one," the young man sitting next to Marc said to him in a low voice. He was a pleasant-looking, clean-cut young man of around 18 years of age, with a well-groomed goatee and a pair of wire-rimmed glasses.

Marc frowned at him. "What are you talking about?"

"Jason, the guy sitting next to your girlfriend."

"Yeah, what about him? He's your friend, isn't he?"

"He was the biggest womaniser at our school, I swear."

Moments later, the sherut shot out of the Ben Gurion Airport security zone and on to the highway, Lisa snugly and smugly sandwiched between Jason the womaniser and Giddy the long-limbed driver with the dancing hands. Marc gritted his teeth and watched the landscape flash past the windscreen at dizzying speeds.

"I'm Barry, by the way," Marc's neighbour announced. Marc looked at him and nodded.

"I'm Marc."

Barry shook his hand. "Where are you two from?"

"Los Angeles," said Marc.

"La La Land?" Barry laughed. "We're from Brooklyn. All three of us. I've never been out west myself." He turned to the sallow young man on his left, the quieter one of the three backpackers. "How about you, Ken? Ever been to California?"

Ken smiled sheepishly at Marc and shook his head no.

"Ken doesn't like to show his teeth," Barry said. "Isn't that right, Kenny?" He cupped his hand around his mouth and said, in an exaggerated mock whisper, "He's been wearing braces on his teeth for years. Embarrassed as hell by them."

"Interesting," Marc said. His stomach was starting to grumble as much from hunger as from aggravation, so he reached into his bag and pulled out a granola bar, tore open the wrapper and bit into it.

As he chewed on the granola bar, he glanced occasionally at the front seat, from which was emanating the sounds of animated but indistinct conversation and occasional explosions of laughter. Lisa's smiling head was pivoting back and forth between her two escorts.

"They make quite a threesome, don't they?" Barry said.

"Spare me the comedy," Marc said, swallowing the last of his granola bar. He looked out of the window. The Tel Aviv suburbs had given way to the open highway. Both sides of the road were bounded by verdant fields of alfalfa.

He glanced at Lisa again out of the corner of his eye. She was determined to spread her wings on this trip regardless of how he felt. *Fine*, he thought. *Hopefully she'll end up flying away and leave me alone.*

"Hey, I'm sorry, man," Barry said. "I didn't mean to offend."

"Forget it."

Barry nodded. "Thanks. So, how long have you two been together, if you don't mind my asking."

"Around two years."

"Wow, long time. I've never lasted even two weeks with anyone. How'd you two meet?"

Marc looked blandly at his inquisitor.

"What's the matter?" Barry said.

"Are you just making conversation or do you really want to know? Because your questions are getting sort of personal," Marc said.

Barry removed his glasses, fogged them up with his breath, and wiped them clean with a corner of his T-shirt. He placed them back on his face and looked at Marc.

"Believe it or not, man, I'm making conversation, and I also want to know," he said, his voice low and serious. "And feel free to ask me personal questions if you want."

"All right," Marc said, nodding at his seatmate, "fair enough. Her father's the cantor at my temple and my father used to be the rabbi."

"Excellent!" Barry said. "A perfect match. Did you hear that, Kenny? These two met at temple."

Kenny nodded and smiled, first at Marc, then at Barry. Marc was beginning to wonder whether the poor guy was some kind of half-wit, when suddenly he opened his mouth and spoke. "You know that Kfar Vered isn't a religious kibbutz, don't you?"

"He's right," Barry said, "far from it. A lot of partying goes on there, if you know what I mean." He offered Marc a salacious smile.

"I'm not planning on being there long," Marc said, shifting uncomfortably.

Lisa spun around in her seat. "What do you mean? We're going to be there for a year."

Marc shrugged. "As long as I can eat kosher and pray on Shabbat, I'll be fine … for the time being."

"Oh, phew," Lisa said, "This is your chance to be free of all those rules that've been put on you since you were born. Experiment a little! Take off that stupid kipa and live it up. It's only a year. If you want to go back to all of it again, you can do it when you go back home. That's my plan anyway."

"Ironic, isn't it?" Marc said to Barry.

"What is?"

"Of all the places in the world to shed her Jewishness, of all the places to spit on the traditions of her ancestors, she wants to do it in Israel."

"Oh, phew," she said and turned back around in her seat. "He can be a real stick-in-the-mud sometimes," she said to her waiting chaperones.

Barry raised his eyebrows at Marc and whispered, "She's a tough one, isn't she? How'd you guys last two years together?"

"It's a long story," Marc said. "Maybe I'll tell you about it sometime."

"Sure thing," Barry said. "Maybe we'll both be assigned to the same chore one day, shovelling cow shit or something. You can tell me all about it then."

"It's a deal."

The big brown sherut drove north along the Mediterranean coast and, as they approached the seaside resort town of Netanya, Giddy pulled over to the shoulder and pointed out a secluded spot next to the highway, where he claimed to have lost his virginity at the age of 13. His detailed account proved to be quite entertaining to all the passengers except Marc, who shook his head and asked Giddy why they were taking the coastal route. It seemed to him that going by an inland route was faster. Giddy ignored the question, ordered his passengers back into the sherut and gunned the engine.

Marc was beginning to feel distressed. He had always imagined Israel would be a palpably spiritual, almost magical place. *The place where the Shekinah glory of the Lord God had dwelt in the midst of men. A place of celebration for the people of God, and a place of reverence.* But up until now, all he had seen of Israel – the disorder, the choking traffic, the tacky taxi driver drooling all over his girlfriend, the seeming absence of respect from most people he'd met so far for the very spirit that created the country – all of this was distressing to Marc.

He stared helplessly out of the window at the passing landscape. The highway was considerably higher than the coastal towns below. And the towns, which were all built at the edge of the deep-blue Mediterranean, shimmered white in the sun.

It was really quite stunning. But, Marc couldn't see it. He was turned inward and feeling miserable.

As they reached Hadera, Giddy shepherded the sherut off the highway and drove into the centre of town. He brought the vehicle to a sudden halt in front of a shabby falafel shop and, leaving the engine running, ran inside. Marc toyed with the idea of hijacking the car. He sat up for a moment and stole a look at the key dangling in the ignition, inadvertently catching sight in the rear-view mirror of Lisa's leg draped over Jason's. Jason was furtively tracing a figure eight on her thigh with the tip of his forefinger. Marc sat back in his seat with a groan and closed his eyes.

"Don't say I didn't warn you," Barry whispered in his ear.

A few minutes later Giddy came out of the falafel shop, his arms laden with paper sacks. He leaned into the sherut, pulled falafel sandwiches and cans of Coke out of the sacks, and distributed them (two sandwiches each) to the passengers. When he had finished passing out the food, he crumpled up the paper sacks, tossed them on to the road and got back into the sherut. The passengers thanked him profusely for his kindness, to which he responded to their astonishment (his mouth stuffed full of falafel mush) that they could reimburse him either now or when they arrived at Kfar Vered.

The sherut's engine roared as Giddy executed a mad U-turn across the road and manoeuvred the vehicle back on to the intercoastal. A few kilometres north of Hadera, the sherut turned on to an inland highway and, to Marc's relief, they left the Mediterranean behind them.

The sherut shot north-east across the upper part of Samaria, through the town of Afula, and onward in the direction of the Galilee. The landscape was becoming progressively greener and hillier as they travelled north. The heavy lunch had made the passengers drowsy and, one by one, they dropped off into a midday slumber, all except Marc. He glanced at Barry. His head was leaning back, his mouth wide open, and Ken's head was resting on his shoulder. Lisa had long ago made herself comfortable against Jason's chest and the two of them were now snoring in sync.

As Marc's eye travelled around the sherut, he caught Giddy studying him in the rear-view mirror. Not to be intimidated, he stared back at him with as hostile a look as he could muster.

After a few moments, Giddy said: "You know, I see a lot of people come through that airport. I know all the types."

Marc leaned forward and spoke directly in Giddy's ear. "What does that have to do with anything? What does that have to do with your disrespecting my girlfriend and me?"

Giddy chuckled and tossed a quick backward glance at Marc. "We're all responsible for our own actions. Me for mine, her for hers, and you for yours. Agreed?"

"Of course, that's obvious."

"Take you, for example," Giddy said. "You're not here to have a good time, are you?"

"Who said?"

"I told you, I know all the types. You're here for different reasons to hers."

"And what reasons are those, pray tell?"

"It's obvious to me. She's a sweet, carefree girl, who probably genuinely loves you, but who is ready to explode into her own womanhood. And you ... you're here for an exorcism, I think."

"Ha, ha," Marc responded.

"Yes, 'ha, ha.' But you won't deny the truth of it, will you?"

Marc looked at Giddy for a moment and shook his head.

"And yet," Giddy said, "knowing that, you still came with her. Whose fault is that? Yours, hers, mine?"

Marc fell back into his seat and crossed his arms. "I don't know," he muttered. "Probably mine."

"Listen, religious boy," Giddy said, "exorcisms don't work. You can go to Safed or to Jerusalem or to the desert, but your demons will follow you wherever you go. Believe me, I know. Better you should stay in Kfar Vered and have yourself some fun. Make a few friends while getting your hands dirty. Yes?"

Marc nodded vaguely, closed his eyes and squeezed the bridge of his nose in an attempt to ward off an advancing migraine. He stayed that way for a while and was eventually lulled to sleep by the vibration of the sherut.

Half an hour later, Giddy called out and woke them out of their naps. He had pulled the sherut off the highway and had gotten out of the car.

The passengers drowsily lifted their heads, blinked at their surroundings, and saw that they were parked on a hill, at some kind of lookout point. Tumbling out of the sherut, they walked to where Giddy was standing. Down below was a lush valley, rich with agriculture, that stretched out for hundreds of kilometres.

"Behold the Hula Valley," Giddy said. "In my opinion, this is the most impressive view in Israel."

"Giddy, my man," Barry said, stretching deliciously, "I wouldn't have thought you were such a romantic."

Giddy smiled at him. "There's more to me than you think."

Marc rolled his eyes and walked to the opposite end of the lookout point. He kicked a stone and watched it bounce down the side of the hill toward the valley below. Lisa sidled up next to him and took his hand. He looked at her for a moment and felt a sad feeling welling up inside.

"What do you want?" he muttered.

"To be with you," she said, rubbing her cheek against his arm.

"Looks more like you want to be with that guy," Marc said, indicating Jason with a lift of his head.

Lisa laughed a bright clear laugh that caught Marc by surprise. "Him? No, no, no, I was only being friendly."

"He was touching your leg. I saw him. And you were letting him."

Lisa let go of Marc's hand and shrugged. "A little flirting never hurt anyone," she said. "Anyway, get over it already. I'm here with you, not him." She touched his nose playfully. "OK?"

Marc smiled weakly and nodded. Lisa pulled him along by the hand to where the others were standing.

"This is a fabulous view," she said to Giddy. Is our kibbutz down there?"

"No, it's on the other side," said Giddy. "Nestled in the hills there." He pointed at a pair of craggy, fog-shrouded hills. "When it's sunny and warm over here, it gets misty all along there." A cryptic smile played across his face. "All right, folks, the break's over. Let's go."

They quickly piled back into the sherut, and Marc and Jason switched places. Lisa and the backpackers spent the rest of their journey animatedly talking about Kfar Vered. They traded rumours they'd heard about their chores. They talked about opportunities to go horseback riding or hiking among the ruins of crusader fortresses in the hills, kayaking on the Jordan River, various weekend sight-seeing possibilities, and the chance to participate in the nightly folklore presentations put on by the kibbutz guesthouse for its visitors.

Marc sat quietly, listening to the exchange. Some of what his fellow travellers were talking about sounded interesting to him, especially the hiking and horseback riding. He had always cherished the few camping experiences he'd had as a child. Participating in the folklore presentations also appealed to him. And by the time the sherut approached the imposing gates of Kfar Vered, Marc was beginning to feel more optimistic about the whole thing. Perhaps having a good time here at Kfar Vered and connecting with his Jewish heritage were not mutually exclusive propositions.

An Israel State of Mind, Part 2

One of the kibbutz security officers ushered Marc, Lisa and the other backpackers into a panelled waiting room where they would soon go through orientation. The room was already occupied by a half dozen other young people, most of them in their teens and early 20s, who were busy mingling with one another, looking at archival photographs displayed on the walls or helping themselves to refreshments. Marc, who was ravenous, broke from his group and approached the refreshment table, which was laid out with vegetarian sandwiches, a chopped tomato and cucumber salad, hummus, pitta, cookies, orange juice and carrot juice. A young woman with daisies braided into her dark blond hair stood behind the table and smiled at him.

"Looks delicious," he said, pointing at the various items of food. "Is it kosher?"

The young woman nodded her head, pointed at the table and continued to smile at Marc. He wondered whether she had understood his question.

"I was wondering if the food is kosher," he said.

"Yes, of course," said the young woman, her smile faltering a bit. "It's kosher … very good. Please eat."

Marc nodded and looked around the room to see if he could find someone else who might reassure him about the food. Next to the exterior door, he spied the security guard who had escorted them engaged in an animated conversation with Giddy, who, for some reason, was still hanging around. Giddy noticed Marc staring at them and said something to the security guard, who disengaged from the conversation and strolled over to Marc.

"Do you need some help?" the guard said.

"Yes, thanks, I'm trying to find out if the food here is kosher."

The guard blinked at Marc and traded a look with the young woman behind the table.

"Did you ask Miriam?" he said, indicating the young woman.

"Yes, I did. I'm not sure she understood me."

"She understands enough. I assume you asked about Kfar Vered's food policy before you signed on?"

Marc was starting to feel like a bug under a microscope.

"Yes, I did ask," he said. "The people at the kibbutz desk assured me that the food was kosher. I only wanted to make sure before I actually ate something."

The security guard looked at Marc with a mystified expression on his face, and exchanged a few words with Miriam in very quick and slangy Hebrew. From Marc's rudimentary knowledge of the language, he was fairly certain they were not discussing the issue he had raised. After a moment, the guard walked away from the table, leaving Marc and Miriam to stare at each other across the food.

Barry and Ken ambled over and began loading up their paper plates with a couple of sandwiches each.

"Hey, man, what's going on?" Barry asked, stuffing the corner of a sandwich into his mouth. "Why aren't you digging in?"

"I don't know," Marc said, picking up a paper plate. He smiled tentatively at Miriam and she returned the smile. "I guess I couldn't make up my mind. How's the sandwich?"

"Good. But you'd better hurry up and eat because the meeting's about to start any second now."

Marc spooned some hummus on to his plate and selected a few pieces of pitta. The chopped salad looked good to him, too, so he transferred a few spoonfuls from the large plastic container to an area on his plate next to the hummus. Grabbing a tall glass, he filled it half with orange juice and half with carrot juice, then he carefully crossed the room and sat in the back row of a group of chairs the staff had set up for the new arrivals.

Lisa snuck up behind him while he ate and pressed her thumbs into his neck. Marc moaned as she worked out a knot right where his neck met his shoulder.

"You're all tense," she said.

Marc nodded painfully.

"You're not still mad at me about that Jason thing, are you?"

"No, not any more," he said, pulling away from her vice-like grip. "You should grab something to eat before they get started."

Hopping into the seat next to him, she snatched a piece of pitta off his plate and smeared it with hummus.

"I wonder where Simon is," she said, holding the pitta thoughtfully a couple of inches in front of her mouth.

"You'd better eat that," Marc said, rubbing the back of his neck and rotating his head to relieve the stiffness. He could still feel the sensation of Lisa's fingers kneading his neck muscles.

Lisa nodded and pushed the pitta into her mouth. Marc ripped his napkin in two and handed half of it to her; Lisa dabbed at her full lips.

"He promised he'd meet us when we got here."

"I'm sure he got held up with his chores or something," Marc said. "Don't worry about it. He's a big boy."

Lisa pushed out her bottom lip in an exaggerated pout, snatched another piece of pitta off Marc's plate and scooped up some of his chopped salad.

"I was so looking forward to seeing him," she said after a moment.

"He'll get here when he gets here."

Suddenly an interior door flew open and a tall, athletic-looking, middle-aged woman marched into the room. A bespectacled, slightly balding gentleman followed her, carrying a notepad and a three-ring binder in his arms. The balding gentleman took a seat at a folding table set up at the front of the room and flipped open the binder. The woman remained standing, legs wide apart, arms akimbo.

As if by command, the young people moved to the chairs and sat down. Barry slipped into the vacant chair next to Marc and left Ken standing alone, a hurt expression darkening his face. Marc placed the half-eaten plate of food underneath his chair and noticed to his chagrin that Jason had taken the seat to Lisa's left.

"Welcome to Kibbutz Kfar Vered," the woman announced, once the room was silent. "My name is Julia Alpern and I am in charge of the English-language volunteers. First, before we begin, Ari, the man seated to my left, will see who is here and who is not."

Ari stood, called the roll and determined that three of the volunteers expected for that day had not arrived. Julia and he conferred for a few moments, after which he returned to his seat.

"All right," Julia continued, "as you heard, we are short a few people. This is normal. People frequently back out at the last minute. This is because they are not fully committed to the volunteer experience. But, we at Kfar Vered prefer that if someone is going to back out that they do so at this stage rather than later on. We are not interested in the uncommitted."

Julia paused dramatically and surveyed the group.

"Very well," she said after a moment, "I would like to welcome you to Kfar Vered, and I trust that your stay here will be everything you expect and more."

Barry nudged Marc with his elbow and flashed a malicious smile at him. "What do you suppose she means by that?" he whispered. Marc shook his head and leaned forward in his chair.

"Some of you will be here for three months, others of you for six months and a couple of you have signed on for a year," she said. "But regardless of the amount of time that you will be here, what you will all have in common are your chores. These will be assigned in rotation on a weekly basis, beginning tomorrow.

"Now, regardless of what you may have heard about our collective, there is much real work to be done here at Kfar Vered. We are both a large kibbutz as well as a functioning three-star guest lodge. Some of you will be assigned to work in the lodge, doing everything from reception to cleaning guest rooms. Others will be assigned to agriculture or to dairy production. Still others will be assigned to general maintenance. But whichever assignment you receive initially, you can be sure you will eventually do everything there is to do here at the kibbutz.

"Of course, not everything is work here at Kfar Vered. You will also have the opportunity to participate in many activities: recreational, educational and social activities. Later on tonight, once you have all settled in, we invite you to attend an informal meeting with the activities coordinator. He will be able to answer all your questions regarding these activities. Are there any questions at this point?"

Marc raised his hand.

"Yes, please tell us your name again, and also tell us where you're from," Julia said.

Marc stood. "I'm Marc Sadot and I'm from Los Angeles."

"Yes, Marc, your question ...?"

Marc looked around the room and noticed for the first time that he was the only person wearing a kipa. He hesitated a moment. Lisa glanced up at him with a puzzled look. After a couple of seconds of silence, all eyes in the room had focused on him.

"Did you forget your question?" Julia asked, glancing at her watch.

"No, I didn't," Marc said, regrouping and focusing on her. "I was going to ask about Shabbat services. Do you have them?"

Julia nodded. "Yes, of course. They're mainly for our guests. You will find that not many of us at Kfar Vered are observant. But if this is not a problem for you, then you will be fine. You will be able to eat kosher here and you can observe Shabbat as you wish. Anybody else?"

Marc took his seat and could feel Lisa's angry eyes on him. He glanced at her, and she returned his look with a deadly glare, her body trembling with rage.

"Why did you ask that?" she whispered. "Now, you're marked."

"What are you talking about 'marked'?"

"Everyone will think you're weird." Tears were beginning to roll down her face.

"Then fuck them," Marc said, and turned away from her.

Suddenly she reached up, yanked off his kipa and stormed out of the room with a loud slam of the door. The other young people in the room exchanged looks and murmured among themselves. Marc calmly reached up, felt the top of his head and removed the dangling hairclips that had formerly held his kipa in place, dropping them into his pocket. Taking advantage of the situation, Ken crept into the now vacant seat between Jason and Marc.

"Wow, that was intense," Barry whispered to Marc. "I can't believe she did that."

"Ladies and gentlemen," Julia said, "may I have your attention again, please. Quiet down, please! Thank you. I'm not exactly sure what just happened but let me say that it is very important, in a cooperative such as ours, that interpersonal issues are not allowed to escalate. Such escalations are disruptive to the work we're trying to do here. Even though we have mechanisms for the resolution of disputes, mechanisms that work quite well, we are sometimes forced to remove individuals from among us when problems become chronic. Are you all clear on this?" Her eyes came to rest on Marc. He nodded in response, as did the others.

"Good, I'm pleased," she said. "And now, at this point, I'm going to turn you over to the person who will be leading you on your tour of the kibbutz facilities. He will also be showing you to your assigned sleeping quarters." She smiled at the doorway and waved.

Marc turned around in his seat and found himself unexpectedly looking at Lisa's brother, Simon. He was dressed in a pair of tight blue jeans and an even tighter faded red T-shirt. Marc's heart leapt into his throat as he watched Simon swagger forward on his powerful legs to join Julia at the front of the room. The past year had agreed with Simon. There was a healthy glow about him and a calm maturity that belied his 21 years. Some of the young women in the group whispered their approval to one another as he moved past.

He greeted Julia with a kiss on both cheeks, then turned and quickly scanned the group. His eyes alighted on Marc for a moment, followed by what seemed to Marc a flicker of recognition. Marc nodded at him and lifted his hand in a wave, but Simon had already turned to Julia and exchanged a few words with her *sotto voce*.

Barry leaned toward Marc and whispered, "Do you know that guy?"

Marc nodded slowly and brought his index finger to his lips as Simon turned again to face the group.

"Hello and welcome. I'm Simon Katz," said Simon, his face serious and unsmiling. A lock of his neck-length hair fell across his right eye and he flipped it back with a flick of his hand. "As Julia mentioned, I'll be showing you around the collective shortly. For the time being, I'd like you all to gather right outside the door and wait for me. I'll join you in about five minutes."

As the group shuffled out of the room, Julia called out: "Marc Sadot, please remain here."

Barry looked questioningly at Marc. "Uh, oh, sounds like trouble. Should I wait for you?"

"No, I'll find you later on, thanks," Marc said.

Barry nodded and ran to catch up with the rest of the group.

Marc approached Julia and Simon, who were discussing something between themselves, and he waited until they both looked at him.

"You wanted to see me about something?"

"Yes," Julia said. "I want you to explain what that episode with the young woman was all about."

Simon stared intently at Marc, and Marc noticed he was holding a crumpled blue kipa in his hands.

"Is that mine?" Marc said, pointing at Simon's hands.

Simon looked at the kipa for a moment and handed it to Marc, who quickly smoothed out the creases.

"Last time I saw you, you were wearing one of these, too," Marc said to Simon once he had resecured the kipa to the top of his head.

"You two know each other?" Julia said, her eyes narrowing.

"We went to the same synagogue for a while," Simon said curtly.

"Oh, for crying out loud," Marc said, "we practically grew up together. What is it with you?"

"Is this true, Simon?" Julia said.

"Yes, it's true," Marc said. "And the young woman who yanked off my kipa is his sister."

Julia scratched her head and looked first at Marc, then at Simon. "You didn't mention this to me before, Simon," she said.

"I didn't think it was relevant."

"You didn't?"

"No. She's a volunteer here like anyone else. Him, too. It's my opinion that whatever relationship may or may not exist between any of us shouldn't matter."

"I see," Julia said. She patted Simon on the shoulder. "Well, it's my opinion that the two of you have some issues to sort out, so I'm going to leave it to the two of you to start discussing them – now." She turned on her heels and walked to the door.

"But, Julia," Simon called out, "what about the tour?"

"I'll get someone else to do it. As for you two, start talking."

And with that, Julia exited the room, leaving Marc and Simon alone.

"Do we hug now or later?" Marc asked with a nervous smile.

Simon grabbed a chair and flopped down into it. "You're fucking funny."

"I wasn't trying to be," Marc said as he dragged a chair over to where Simon was sitting. "After all, we've done a lot more than that back home."

"Don't go there, all right?"

"Don't go there?" Marc laughed bitterly. "You're the one who's been hopping into my bed for the past six years. So don't tell me not to go there."

Simon looked around the room and shook his head. "Look, I'm sorry about all that, OK? It's in the past now." He pumped his legs nervously.

Marc scooted his chair closer to Simon and lowered his voice. "It may be in the past for you, but it has messed me up real good in the *here and now*. You get what I'm saying? Sometimes I'm not even sure which end is up any more."

Simon got to his feet and moved away from Marc. "So now what – you're planning on stalking me for the rest of my goddamned life?"

"What are you talking about?"

"I mean, what are you fucking doing here? At my kibbutz? Out of all the kibbutzim in Israel, you had to come here."

Marc burst out laughing. It was the first good laugh he'd had in a long time. He laughed so hard that the tears stood out in his eyes and his sides began to throb.

"Stop that!" said Simon.

"Oh my God," Marc said, after recovering his composure and wiping his face with his sleeve, "you think I came here because of you?"

"Well, why the hell else? Who else do you know here?"

Marc laughed some more and then patted Simon's chair. "Sit down and I'll tell you all about it."

Simon crossed his arms. "I can hear you just as well standing as I can sitting."

"Sit down, will you?" Marc said. "I promise I won't maul you."

Simon's head snapped in the direction of the kitchen.

"What is it?" Marc said.

"Be quiet," Simon whispered. "I thought I heard something."

Marc watched as Simon moved stealthily toward the kitchen door, slowly pushed it open and stepped inside. After a moment, he came back into the room, shaking his head.

"I could swear I heard something," he said.

"I didn't hear anything."

"Well, I did. Or at least I thought I did." Simon moved absently to the chair and dropped into it. "Anyway, I'm sitting now. So, what's the story?"

The fact that Simon sat down made Marc feel a little better, made him feel some of the closeness he used to feel with Simon when they were younger. He flashed a smile. "OK, so this is how it goes. My original plan was to spend a year alone in Israel following graduation from high school, partly to get away from home, and partly to work out some personal problems I've been having."

Simon nodded. "Personal problems, eh?"

"Yeah, personal, you know, as in confusion about my sexuality – thanks to you – and other stuff. So I thought I might try a religious kibbutz or someplace like that to try to work things out. To try to get cured of my problems."

Simon shook his head. "OK, fine, you're here to get cured, whatever. So how did you and Lisa end up here at Kfar Vered?"

"That was an annoying fluke, actually. I didn't want her to come with me. What happened was that when I mentioned to my mother that I wanted to go to Israel for a year, she didn't think it was a good idea for me to go alone."

"Of course not."

"Right, so she ended up ringing your mom and, before I knew it, all the arrangements had been made for Lisa and me to come here and join you. So you see, I never had any intention of coming here and bothering you."

Simon looked down at his palms for a moment, then brushed them briskly against his legs. "I don't suppose you've discussed any of this with Lisa?"

"Not at all. She doesn't have a clue."

"Are you sure about that?" Simon tapped Marc's kipa with his finger. "She was pretty upset when I ran into her outside. She says you're trying to push her away."

"Apparently, it doesn't take much," Marc said with a shake of his head. "Ever since we got here she's been throwing herself at almost every guy she sees."

Simon stood. "Well, I think, for the time being, the two of you should keep the hell out of each other's way. To keep the peace."

Marc nodded and held out his hand to Simon. "Don't worry, I'll clear out of here as soon as I can make arrangements. I don't want to be a nuisance to you."

Simon regarded Marc's outstretched hand for a moment, then shook it without much enthusiasm. "Don't worry about that. I guess you don't have to leave if you don't want to." He pulled an elastic band out of his pocket and pulled back his hair into a short ponytail. "Anyway, I think we've finished sorting out our issues, don't you?"

Marc shrugged. "Not really. I think there's a lot more we could talk about, you being the experienced older guy and all."

Simon's face became dead serious. "I'm sorry, but that is the best I can do, at least for now."

Marc stared at him and Simon returned the stare with his clear brown eyes. It had been a year since Marc had stared into those eyes. He allowed himself to study Simon's handsome face, the high cheekbones, the Roman nose, the full lower lip and powerful chin, and he felt a sudden desire to hold him close. It was at that moment that Marc realised what he had never truly realised before: he was utterly in love with Simon. This realisation was almost more than he could bear. He had come to Israel in the hopes of ridding himself of these desires, to finally know himself as heterosexual. But his encounter with Simon had destroyed all hopes of that.

"Simon," he said, moving toward him, "do you think we could –?"

Simon halted Marc's forward movement by placing a hand on his shoulder and holding him at arm's length. "No, we can't."

"But –"

"Sorry, man, I can't." Simon glanced at his watch. "Shit, I've got to run." He looked back at Marc. "Are you sure you'll be all right?"

Marc shrugged his shoulders and nodded, and Simon bounded across the room and out of the door. Marc waited a moment, then walked to the window and drew aside the curtain. He watched Simon dashing down a flagstone-paved walkway and felt a dull ache in the pit of his stomach and a tightness in his throat. He felt foolish and humiliated for having suggested anything to Simon. And Simon's abrupt rejection made him feel even worse. Marc watched sadly as Simon reached the bottom of the path, turned the corner and disappeared from view around a Quonset hut.

Somewhere outside a steam whistle screamed and the sound was reflected back from the surrounding hills. Seconds later, small groups of kibbutzniks and volunteers began streaming out of the various buildings, chattering enthusiastically in different languages and heading off on the flagstone footpaths to the different parts of the kibbutz.

Marc frowned, let the curtain drop back into place and sat down heavily on an old beaten-up leather couch. The sounds of lively conversation outside contrasted sharply with the tomblike silence of the room and made him feel lonelier than he had ever felt before in his entire life. He let out a sigh and was about to lie back on the sofa when he was startled by a shuffling sound behind him. Turning around, he caught sight of a pair of brown penny loafers disappearing behind a partition on the other side of the room. He slid off the sofa, crept over to the partition and yanked it aside, exposing an embarrassed-looking Ken.

"What are you doing here?" Marc said, narrowing his eyes.

Ken flashed a sheepish smile and covered his mouth with one hand to hide his braces.

"Come on," Marc said, taking the shy young man gently by the arm and drawing him out of the shadows, "out with it."

"It was all Barry's idea," Ken said, softly. "He thought you should have a witness or something, just in case."

"In case what?"

Ken shrugged his shoulders.

"That was you in the kitchen earlier?" Marc said, letting go of his arm.

Ken smiled and nodded. "That guy, Simon, he almost caught me but I was able to roll under the sink in the nick of time."

Marc blinked at Ken. "How long were you in there?"

"I'm not sure," he said. "But I heard everything you guys said, if that's what you want to know."

Marc stared wide-eyed at Ken and felt as if an intense pressure were being applied to his solar plexus. He forgot to breathe for a few seconds and began to feel light-headed. The secret he had guarded for so long from everybody had been finally discovered by a virtual stranger. Thrusting out a hand to steady himself against the wall, he gasped for breath. Ken stretched out his hand to touch his shoulder, but Marc shook it off and backed away from him.

"Don't worry," Ken said, "I won't tell anyone."

Marc forced himself to take slow and steady breaths. He told himself that somehow he had to take charge of the situation. With each deep breath that he drew, he felt his panic subsiding; in its place, a smouldering anger began to take over: anger at Ken for eavesdropping on his conversation and anger at Simon for having created the situation in the first place. But angry as he was, he wanted to avoid making an enemy out of Ken for fear he might spread the details of the conversation he had overheard. He stared long and hard at Ken.

"Please, Ken," he said, his voice hoarse with emotion, "you must promise me that you'll never repeat any of what you heard to anyone."

Ken nodded vigorously. "I promise." A grin spread on his face, and his hand automatically came up and hovered in front of his mouth. "This will be our secret."

Marc looked away from Ken. He slowly raked his fingers through his hair, pulling off his kipa in the process and stuffing it into his pocket. He stumbled to the sofa, slipped on his backpack and walked zombie-like toward the door.

Ken glided up behind Marc as he stepped outside and stood on the porch of the meeting hall, which was perched on a hill overlooking the rest of the kibbutz. They stood blinking in the glare of the bright sunlight of the late afternoon. After a moment, Ken tapped Marc on the shoulder.

"What is it, Ken?" Marc said.

"Do you want to talk about it? About what I heard in there?"

Marc stared at him. There was an odd look of anxiety on Ken's face that belied his ever-present smile, and it made Marc feel uneasy. He pushed it out of his mind for the moment.

"I'd rather not," Marc said finally. "At least not now."

He looked down at the kibbutz grounds with a shake of his head. From where they were standing, they had a clear westward view of an orange grove that had been planted down the side of one of the hillsides. The sweet scent of orange blossom was borne to them on a warm breeze. Marc pulled off his pack and took in a deep breath. The smell of orange blossom reminded him of a warm spring afternoon in Southern California. He sat on a low retaining wall made of concrete blocks and closed his eyes. Ken looked at him curiously for a moment and sat next to him.

A few minutes later, Julia appeared at the bottom of the main path and bounded up the hill in their direction, taking two steps at a time without breaking a sweat. As she drew closer, Ken waved her down. Julia slowed her pace, approached them, and opened her mouth to speak. But Ken placed his index finger against his lips and pointed at Marc. Julia nodded, then crept forward and lowered herself on to the retaining wall to Marc's left. Sensing her presence, Marc opened one eye and looked at her.

"Were you and Simon able to sort things out?" she said.

Marc opened both eyes and drew himself up a bit. "Sure, we talked. Don't worry, you won't get any problems from me."

Ken leaned forward and stared at Julia from across Marc's chest. She nodded at him and forced a smile. "Do you mind showing us to our accommodations?" he said.

Julia looked thoughtfully at Ken and then at Marc. After a moment, she stood and slapped off the dirt and twigs that had adhered to the back of her slacks. "Tell me," she said to Ken, "how is it you missed the tour? I don't recall seeing you with the rest of the group."

"He stayed behind to wait for me," said Marc, standing up abruptly. He tottered on the edge of the wall. Ken held out a hand to steady his legs. "I asked him to stay," he continued.

Ken nodded. "So, do you think we could get going, Miss? I'm exhausted."

"Yes, please," Marc chimed in, "I'd like to get out of these travelling clothes and shower before dinner."

"Certainly," said Julia, "I'll find someone to show you the way. Wait here." She moved toward the meeting hall, halted and turned back toward them. "Oh, by the way, Mr Sadot," she said, "Lisa Katz is in bunkhouse number eight … in case you were wondering."

Marc nodded. "Thank you," he said, as Julia disappeared into the meeting hall. Marc stared at the door for a moment.

"So you and Lisa are broken up now, aren't you?" Ken said.

"I don't know," Marc said quietly, turning back to the view. "I guess we'll know soon enough."

A second steam whistle screamed in the distance, setting into motion another exodus of workers from the various buildings. The young people marched down both hills toward the narrow valley below. Ken smiled to see them scurrying down the various paths in the reddening light of the late afternoon. Shielding his eyes with one hand, Marc squinted as the rays of the sun, now almost perpendicular to where they were standing, cast long black shadows behind them against the meeting hall.

It took only a few minutes more for the sun to drop below the horizon. A heavy mist began to rise from the wheat fields below and a bank of low rolling clouds crept in over the hills. Within a few short minutes, thick roiling fog obscured their view of the kibbutz.

A brisk wind kicked down the sides of the hills, rustling leaves and reddening their faces. Marc fished a light jacket out of his pack and Ken sat down on the ground and hugged his knees.

"I'm hungry," Ken said.

Just then, the echo of light footsteps reflected off the walls of the surrounding buildings. The footsteps seemed to be moving up the path in their direction. Ken stood and peered into the fog as a vague figure materialised in front of them. Marc stepped forward in time to see the figure resolve itself into the person of Miriam, the food monitor from earlier, an Uzi sub-machine gun slung casually over her shoulder. She approached them with a friendly smile.

"That is one dangerous-looking purse you've got there," Marc said, pointing at the weapon.

"Purse?" she said, searching for the phantom purse.

Ken broke into a nervous giggle. Miriam's head snapped up and looked from one to the other.

"I was talking about the Uzi," Marc said, still pointing.

Miriam crinkled her brow, drew the gun around, and regarded it. "But you said 'purse'?"

Marc dropped his hand and smiled at her. "It was only a little joke. You were wearing the gun the way some women wear their purses ..."

Miriam thought about it for a moment, looked at the gun again, and slung it back over her shoulder with a slight shrug. "My name is Miriam," she said finally, extending her hand to Marc.

"Yes, I know," Marc said, "we met earlier in there." He jerked a thumb in the direction of the meeting hall. "You don't remember?"

"Sure, I remember," she said, drawing back her hand a bit. "But, you didn't tell me your name."

"Right, sorry. I'm Marc," he said, stepping forward and pumping her hand. He nodded at Ken. "This is my friend Ken."

"Hello, Marc ... hello, Ken."

Ken shook Miriam's hand. "We're waiting for our escort," he said, "in case you're wondering what we're doing here."

Miriam laughed and began to walk away from them. Marc and Ken exchanged a glance, then looked back at her as she moved a little way down the fog-shrouded path. "I'm your escort," she called out over her shoulder. "Follow me."

Jerusalem Ablaze

The darkness was total and the room seemed formless and void. The young priest lay naked on his side, staring into the black. Next to him he could hear the rustling of a person moving about. The air was heavy with a woman's perfume.

"What's your name?" he asked.

There was a moment of pause. He felt the bed lean in the direction of a new weight as the person sat next to him.

"I'm the woman your father warned you about."

The young man laughed half-heartedly.

"He never warned me."

"I guess that explains why you got caught."

There was something unpleasant about the woman's voice. It was husky, edged with bitterness. The young priest found the darkness of the room depressing.

"Listen," he said, "couldn't we light a candle or something?"

"It's better in the dark. Your senses are keener. You can feel what's happening to you better in the dark."

"Oh."

The woman laughed quietly to herself. Then she spoke again: "And God said, 'Let there be light,' and there was light."

There was a loud snap as she struck a match; the blaze of its flame cast a dim glow on the woman's face. She was ghastly in the flickering light.

"You want a cigarette?"

"No, thank you. I don't smoke."

"It figures," she said, lighting a cigarette. She took a couple of initiatory drags and blew out the match.

The young priest could see the glowing end of the cigarette floating in the darkness, sometimes faintly; at other times, it seemed angrily to come alive.

"You shouldn't blaspheme like that," he said.

"When did I blaspheme?"

"You know … when you lit the match."

"Oh, that," the woman said. "Why? Does it bother you?"

"Yes, it does. It should bother you, too."

"Well it doesn't. Why'd you follow me here?"

"I don't know. I've been thinking about it for a while but I never thought I'd ever do it."

"Thinking about it for a while, eh? How long is a while?"

"About two months, I suppose. That's when you started hanging around in the streets outside the church. I first noticed you as I looked out of the chapel window. You were leaning against that statue of Saint Francis. Later, you seemed to pop up everywhere."

"Yeah, I like to watch you and the other priest boys parading down the street in your little black uniforms. It turns me on. I'd give it to you all for free, if you'd ask me for it. But, you … you're the one who stood out from the rest of them."

"Really?"

"Yeah, really. You've got a real lusty eye."

The young priest felt the blood rush into his face.

"Every time I passed your little group, I could feel you stripping me with your eyes." She leaned over and whispered into his ear, "Your lust-filled eyes."

There was a long silence. The young priest felt the woman lean over the edge of the bed. She seemed to be picking up something off the floor.

"The archbishop … he calls you 'that crimson harlot,'" he said, imitating the archbishop's Greek accent.

"Crimson harlot? Jesus Christ, is he from the Stone Age or what? Sure you don't want a cigarette?"

"No, thank you."

The woman lit another cigarette. The air in the room was becoming fetid and the young priest was feeling the beginnings of nausea.

"Would it be all right if we got started?" he asked.

"Don't rush me. OK?"

"Sorry."

"What's your name?"

"David."

"David what?"

"Mizrahi. David Mizrahi."

"What the hell kind of name's that for a Catholic priest?"

"I was born Jewish."

"No shit? So was I."

"You were? Where are you from?"

"San Francisco. I've only been here a year."

"Your Hebrew's not bad."

"Yeah, well ... How about you? Are you a native?"

"Yes, I'm originally from Mitspe Ramon."

"You mean that little clay mining town in the middle of the desert?"

"Yes. Have you been there?"

"God, what a hellhole!"

"I like it."

"I hate the desert. It's a terrible place. Just a bunch of Bedouins pissing in caves. Have you ever pissed in a cave?"

"There aren't that many caves."

"In a cave, under rocks, right out in the open, what the hell difference does it make? It's a terrible place."

"Actually, it's quite beautiful. Our town overlooks this absolutely amazing crater –"

"I know, I've been there, remember? What's so beautiful about it?"

"I don't know ... It's a feeling I get when I stand at the edge of the crater." He smiled to himself. "The quality of light makes everything look surreal. It's a landscape straight out of science fiction – ochre and black patterns, jagged, twisting and massive shapes. In late afternoon the sun splashes the whole scene with an eerie red colour. Sometimes I imagine I'm looking at the earth the way it looked 50 million years ago."

"My, aren't we poetic."

"I miss it."

"I spent quite a bit of time in the desert myself."

"When was that?"

"After I'd been here about six months. Someone told me I could hook up with some Bedouins down in Beersheba. You know, Arab hospitality and all that."

"So, what happened?"

"I met this family who agreed to take me around in exchange for English lessons."

"Sounds exciting."

"It was the shits. We wandered around for about a month. It was hell. I thought I was going to lose my mind. After two weeks, I was sick of the food, sick of the smell, sick of their ugly faces, sick, sick, sick! One day, I wandered from the camp and laid myself down on the top of a hill, naked."

"Why'd you do that?"

"I wanted the sun to evaporate me, I don't know. The point is, I did it. There were these giant red ants running around on that hill and I let them crawl all over me. I let them bite me. I swear, they probably would've eaten me alive if I'd let them."

"How terrible."

The woman laughed quietly.

"It felt good."

Her words hung in the long silence that followed. They seemed to thicken in the darkness of the room.

"I beg your pardon?

"I said it felt good."

"Ants eating you alive felt good?"

"You've heard that old saying, 'There's a fine line between pleasure and pain,' haven't you?"

"Yes, of course. But –"

"It's all true. If you convince yourself something feels good, then different kinds of pain can provide opportunities for new and unique kinds of pleasure."

"I don't believe that."

"Here, let me show you."

He felt the weight of the bed shift in his direction as the woman leaned over him. Her pendulous breasts dangled on his chest. Suddenly two hands grabbed hold of his hair.

"Hey! What the –"

"Relax and concentrate."

The hands gripped his hair firm and steady.

"How does it feel? Does it hurt?"

"No … not too much."

"Does it feel good?"

"Well …"

"Does it or doesn't it?"

"Well, in a way it does."

"Good. Now I'm going to pull a little harder."

"Ah!"

"Does it hurt?"

"Yes!"

"Wait a second, then tell me."

The pain receded into a comfortable numbness as his scalp adjusted to the increased pressure.

"How is it now?"

"It's all right. Listen, do you think we could get started?"

"Just a little more."

The hands yanked hard on his hair, sending a sharp pain through his head.

"Hey, you're going to pull it out!"

"There, I'm done. See, it wasn't all bad, was it?"

"No … yes … I don't know. Please, we have to hurry. I'll be missed."

"We have plenty of time."

"No, really –"

Outside, the heavy footsteps of the midnight sentry echoed through the alley. The young priest felt the woman's body tense.

"What's wrong?" he said.

"Shut up for a minute."

"It's only the –"

"I said shut up, God damn you!"

The footsteps marched past the door and continued down the alley. The woman didn't move until they had faded away into the stillness of the night. When she spoke again, her voice sounded different. It seemed to come from much deeper within her body.

"Here, eat this."

"What is it?"

He felt a cold hand force open his mouth and a pair of fingers stick something slimy between his teeth. He struggled but the woman was strong, very strong.

"Jesus Christ, God Almighty ... what the hell is that?"

"Chew!"

He felt the object in his mouth oozing some kind of jellylike substance.

"Now, swallow it."

He tried to swallow, but the object kept coming up as he was overcome by a fit of gagging. Rolling on his side he spat the thing out over the edge of the bed. He felt the weight of the woman abruptly shift in his direction and a hand pull him back again.

"Now that wasn't very nice." The woman drew a deep breath. "Don't worry, I've got one more."

"No, please ... No, thank you ..."

"What's wrong?" she said, "You're not nervous, are you?"

"I'm going to be sick."

The young priest leaned once again over the side of the bed and was taken with a fit of dry heaves. *God is punishing me*, he thought. He felt himself jerked back.

"Shall we get started?" he heard the woman's voice say.

"Yes … yes. Please, let's get this over with."

"What's your rush … we've got all night."

"No. I told you, I've got to get back."

"Oh, all right. Say, this isn't your first time, is it?"

The musk of the prostitute's sweat and heavy perfume made the young priest nauseous and dizzy.

"Yes … my first."

"You've got to be fucking joking. Why, I'll bet you're as big a *mamzer* as they come."

"No, honest … my first time."

"Hmmm. Here, I've got an idea. I could tie you down."

"Why would you do that?"

"Listen to me, it's perfect. Can't you see? I'll tie you down! Let me do all the work; all you have to do is lie there."

"I don't know …"

He wanted to run, to go back to his parents, to God, and ask their forgiveness but something told him it was too late. Somehow he knew he had already lost the world to come.

"Go ahead," he said, letting himself be tied, arms and legs, one to each of the four posts of the bed. A sadness crept over him and he began weeping.

"What's wrong with you?"

"Nothing … nothing, please don't ask me."

"You feel guilty about this, don't you?"

"I was a Jew, then I became a Catholic. I really let down my family … now I'm just damned."

"Aw, you poor Judas. Here, let's see if this makes you feel any better."

He felt a cold edge of steel being drawn across his stomach, accompanied by a strange tickling sensation as a warmth spread down his side.

"Hey, lady, what's the matter with you? Why'd you cut me?"

"You've heard the scripture, 'without the shedding of blood there is no remission of sin'?"

"What about it?"

"I've absolved you."

"Please ... please don't say things like that."

"Now that your sins are forgiven, we can begin."

He felt the woman's hands grope his body, starting at his chest and moving downward. One cold hand took hold of him tightly by the groin.

"Why, you are Jewish, through and through," she said with mock amazement.

Pain shot from his testicles into his abdomen.

"Would you please let go?"

"Why? Does it hurt?"

"No ... just let go."

The hand released him from its grip.

"All right," the woman said, "let's get started."

She moved over him and straddled his body. He slipped easily into her. She moved steadily, up and down on him. At one point he thought he had felt this sensation before. She stopped for a moment to light a cigarette, and then continued. The glow of the cigarette moving wildly in the darkness seemed to him like a stick of incense being wielded by an invisible spirit. The woman's breathing was hoarse, and he noticed his own breathing taking on the same rhythm as the woman's. She rode him more vigorously until an incredible rush brought his semen to the boiling point.

"Are you close?" the woman gasped.

"Very!"

"Tell me when."

"Now!" he said.

In the midst of his climax he saw the burning end of the cigarette move toward him and felt its hot sting bite into his skin, right below his armpit. He bit his lip against the pain. *I deserve this*, he thought.

He lay on the bed, breathing hard, the woman's weight still hot around his groin. Ever so slowly, he felt himself slide out of her as she gradually lifted herself off him.

"There, now, did you like that?" she whispered into his ear.

The ropes were cutting his wrists.

"Yes … it was all right. Please, untie me now."

"Untie you? No, I'd never do something like that."

"For the love of God, lady. Let me loose. I've got to go."

He heard her unpleasant laugh once again.

"I can't untie you yet."

The woman leaned close to his head. He felt the rough texture of a canvas-like strap being drawn tight across his mouth as she worked fast to gag him.

"I can't untie you. We've only just started."

—⁂—

The sun burst over the Judean Hills, setting Jerusalem ablaze. On the top of Mount Scopus, a visiting professor stepped out on to the balcony of his office and lit his pipe. He looked down at the walls of the Old City and mused about the way it seemed to glow. Down below, Arab shopkeepers busily worked to open their little shops. The marketplace was filling with the sights, sounds and smells of the bustling city. The early-morning sentry wound its way down narrow alleys, past the small flats, churches, shrines, coffee shops and synagogues.

The sun's rays pushed westward, filling every corner they could find with their radiance. They poured into a certain small room, as the window blinds were flung open by a dishevelled, middle-aged woman. She moved to a large dresser, which sat at the opposite end of the room.

On the bed a naked young man lay on his back, his eyes fixed rigidly on the ceiling – his head encrusted with blood, his mouth slightly open. His body, now forever still, bore the wounds of last night's passions. On the floor lay a heap of black clothing and a few discarded lengths of rope.

The woman pulled on a bright-red knitted dress that barely reached the middle of her thighs. She peered closely at herself in the mirror as she hurriedly applied her makeup, never bothering to brush out her mane of black hair. Grabbing her purse, she moved to the figure on the bed. She leaned over and passionately kissed the young man's bluish lips. Then, slinging her purse over her shoulder, she moved to the door and – blowing a kiss at the mezuzah – stepped out of the doorway and into the sun.